W9-CJM-711

PUFFIN BOOKS
PIPPI GOES ON BOARD

Pippi Longstocking is the little girl with such a rol-
licking, unusual way of looking at things that she
had no difficulty whatsoever in living without grownups—especially as her father (who unfortunately
blew off his ship one day and disappeared) has given
her a suitcase full of gold.

Pippi's next-door neighbors, Tommy and Annika,
find life with Pippi so fascinating—like getting shipwrecked, or going shopping for six pints of assorted
medicines and thirty-six pounds of candy—that when
her father suddenly reappears to take her off to sea,
they are miserable. But Pippi, the hilarious daredevil
with strength enough to lift her own horse when
necessary, can also be gentle and generous, and so
she makes an unexpected decision.

OTHER BOOKS ABOUT PIPPI ARE

Pippi Longstocking
Pippi in the South Seas

Pippi Goes on Board

Astrid Lindgren

Translated by Florence Lamborn
Illustrated by Louis S. Glanzman

Buccaneer Books
Cutchogue, New York

International Standard Book Number: 0-89967-014-8

For ordering information, contact:

Buccaneer Books, Inc.
P.O. Box 168
Cutchogue, N.Y. 11935

(516) 734-5724, Fax (516) 734-7920

- A Limited Edition of 400 Copies -

Contents

Pippi Goes on Board

1
Pippi at Home
in Villa
Villekulla

If a stranger should come to a certain little Swedish town and should happen one day to find himself at a certain spot on the edge of it, he would see Villa Villekulla. Not that the cottage is much to look at— it's rather a ramshackle old place with a tangled garden around it. But it would be natural for a stranger to pause and wonder who lived there, and why there was a horse on the porch. If it was evening and beginning to get dark, and if he caught a glimpse of a little girl strolling around in the garden looking as if she had no idea of going to bed, he might think, "Now I wonder why that little girl's mother doesn't see that she goes to bed? All the other children are fast asleep by this time of night."

If the little girl came to the gate—as she would almost certainly do, because she liked talking to people—then he would be able to take a good look at her. And he would very likely think, "She's one of the most freckled and red-haired children I've ever seen." Later on he would probably think, "Freckles and red hair are really very nice—that is, if the person who has them looks as happy as this child does."

Any stranger would probably be interested to know the name of this little redhead sauntering around by herself in the twilight, and he would ask, "What's your name?"

And she'd answer gaily, "My name's Pippilotta Delicatessa Windowshade Mackrelmint Efraim's Daughter Longstocking, daughter of Captain Efraim Longstocking, formerly the Terror of the Sea, now a cannibal king. But everybody calls me Pippi."

She really believed it when she said her father was a cannibal king, because he had once been blown overboard and had vanished from sight when he and Pippi were sailing on the sea. Pippi's father was rather stout, so she was sure he couldn't have drowned. It was perfectly reasonable to think that he had been washed up on an island and become king of the cannibals there. This is what Pippi was sure must have happened.

If the stranger went on talking with Pippi, he would learn that Pippi lived all alone at Villa Ville-kulla—alone, that is, except for the horse on the porch and a monkey called Mr. Nilsson. If he was a kindhearted man, he would naturally wonder, How does this poor youngster live?

But he needn't have worried. "I'm rich as a troll," Pippi used to say. And she was. She had a whole suitcase full of gold pieces that her father had given her, and she got along beautifully with neither a father nor a mother. Because there was nobody there to tell her when to go to bed, Pippi told herself. Sometimes, to be sure, she didn't tell herself until around ten o'clock, because she had never been able to see why children *should* go to bed at seven. After seven was when you could have the most fun. So the stranger shouldn't have been surprised to see Pippi roaming around the garden even after the sun had gone down and the air was getting cold and Tommy and Annika had been tucked into bed long ago.

Tommy and Annika were the children Pippi played with. They lived next door. They had both a father and a mother, and both father and mother thought it was a good thing for children to go to bed at seven.

If the stranger stayed after Pippi had said good night and gone away from the gate, and if he saw Pippi go up on the porch and pick up the horse in her strong arms and carry him out into the garden, he would certainly rub his eyes and wonder if he were dreaming.

"What an extraordinary child this is!" he would say to himself. "Why, she can actually lift that horse! She's the most extraordinary child I've ever seen!"

He'd be right, too. Pippi *was* the most extraordinary child—in that town, at any rate. There *may* be more extraordinary children in other places, but in that little town there was no one to compare with Pippi Longstocking. And nowhere in the world, in that town or any other, was there anyone half so strong as she was.

2
Pippi Goes Shopping

One lovely spring day when the sun was shining, the birds were singing, and water was running in all the ditches, Tommy and Annika came skipping over to Pippi's. Tommy had brought along a couple of lumps of sugar for Pippi's horse, and both he and Annika stopped on the porch to pat the horse before they went into the house. Pippi was asleep with her feet on the pillow and her head way under the covers. That was the way she always slept.

Annika pinched Pippi's big toe and said, "Wake up!"

Mr. Nilsson was already awake and had jumped up and seated himself on the overhead light. Something began to stir under the quilts, and suddenly a red head popped out. Pippi opened her bright eyes and smiled broadly. "Oh, it's you pinching my toes? I thought it was my father, the cannibal king, looking to see if I had any corns."

She sat down on the edge of the bed and pulled on her stockings—one brown and one black.

"No, sir, you'll never get corns as long as you wear these," she said, and thrust her feet into her large black shoes, which were exactly twice as long as her feet.

"Pippi," said Tommy, "what shall we do today? Annika and I don't have any school."

"Well, now, that's worth thinking about," said Pippi. "We can't dance around the Christmas tree because we threw it out three months ago. Otherwise we could have dashed around on the ice all morning long. Gold-digging would be fun, but we can't do that either because we don't know where to dig. Furthermore, most of the gold is in Alaska, where there are so many gold-diggers already that there wouldn't be room for us. No, we'll have to think of something else."

"Yes, something jolly," said Annika.

Pippi braided her hair into two tight braids that stuck straight out. She considered.

"How would it be if we went into town and did some shopping?" she said at last.

"But we haven't any money," said Tommy.

"I have," said Pippi, and to prove it she opened her suitcase, which of course was chock full of gold pieces. She carefully scooped up a good handful and put them into her apron pocket, which was just exactly in the middle of her stomach.

"If I only had my hat now, I'd be all ready to start," she said. The hat was nowhere to be seen. Pippi looked first in the woodbox, but, remarkable as it may seem, the hat was not there. Then she looked in the bread crock in the pantry, but there were only a garter, a broken alarm clock, and a little bread. At last she even looked on the hat shelf, but there was nothing there except a frying pan, a screwdriver, and a piece of cheese.

"There's no order here at all, and you can't find a single thing," said Pippi disgustedly, "though to be sure I have missed this piece of cheese for a long time and it's lucky it turned up at last.

"Hey, Hat," she shrieked, "are you going shopping or aren't you? If you don't come out this minute it will be too late."

No hat came out.

"Well, then, it can blame itself if it's so stupid, but when I get home I don't want to hear any complaining," she said sternly.

A few minutes later they were marching down the road to town—Tommy, Annika, and Pippi with Mr. Nilsson on her shoulder. The sun was shining so gloriously, the sky was so blue, and the children were so happy! And in the gutter along the roadside the water flowed merrily by. It was a very deep gutter with a great deal of water in it.

"I love gutters," said Pippi and without giving much thought to the matter, she stepped into the water. It reached way over her knees, and if she skipped along briskly it splattered Tommy and Annika.

"I'm making believe I'm a boat," she said, plowing through the water. Just as she spoke she stumbled and went under.

"Or, to be more exact, a submarine," she continued calmly when she got her nose in the air again.

"Oh, Pippi, you're absolutely soaked," said Annika anxiously.

"And what's wrong with that?" asked Pippi. "Is there a law that children should always be dry? I've heard it said that cold showers are very good for the health. It's only in this country that people have got the notion that children shouldn't walk in gutters. In America the gutters are so full of children that there is no room for the water. They stay there the year round. Of course in the winter they freeze in and their heads stick up through the ice. Their mothers have to carry fruit soup and meatballs to them because they can't come home for dinner. But they're sound as nuts, you can be sure of that."

The little town looked pleasant and comfortable in the spring sunshine. The narrow cobblestone streets wound in and out every which way among the houses. Almost every house was surrounded by a little yard in which snowdrops and crocuses were peeping up. There were a good many shops in the town, and on this lovely spring day so many people were running in and out that the bells on the shop doors tinkled unceasingly. The ladies came with baskets on their arms to buy coffee and sugar and soap and butter. Some of the children were also out to buy candy or chewing gum. Most of them, however, had no money for shopping, and the poor dears had to stand outside the shops and just look in at all the good things in the windows.

When the day was at its sunniest and brightest, three little figures appeared on Main Street. They were Tommy and Annika and Pippi—a very wet Pippi, who left a little trickle of water in her path.

"Aren't we lucky, though?" said Annika. "Look at all the shops, and we have a whole apron pocket full of gold pieces!"

Tommy was so happy when he thought of this that he gave a high skip.

"Well, let's get going," said Pippi. "First of all I want to buy myself a piano."

"But, Pippi," said Tommy, "you can't play the piano, can you?"

"How can I tell," said Pippi, "when I've never

tried? I've never had any piano to try on. And this much I can tell you, Tommy—to play the piano without any piano, that takes a powerful lot of practicing."

There didn't seem to be any piano store. Instead the children came to a perfume shop. In the show window was a large jar of freckle salve, and beside the jar was a sign which read: DO YOU SUFFER FROM FRECKLES?

"What does the sign say?" ask Pippi. She couldn't read very well because she didn't want to go to school as other children did.

"It says, 'Do you suffer from freckles?'" said Annika.

"Does it indeed?" said Pippi thoughtfully. "Well, a civil question deserves a civil answer. Let's go in."

She opened the door and entered the shop, closely followed by Tommy and Annika. An elderly lady stood back of the counter. Pippi went right up to her. "No!" she said decidedly.

"What is it you want?" asked the lady.

"No," said Pippi once more.

"I don't understand what you mean," said the lady.

"No, I don't suffer from freckles," said Pippi.

Then the lady understood, but she took one look at Pippi and burst out, "But, my dear child, your whole face is covered with freckles!"

"I know it," said Pippi, "but I don't suffer from them. I love them. Good morning."

She turned to leave, but when she got to the door she looked back and cried, "But if you should happen to get in any salve that gives people more freckles, then you can send me seven or eight jars."

Next to the perfume store was a shop that sold ladies' clothes.

"So far we haven't done much shopping," said Pippi. "Now we must really get going."

And they tramped into the store—first Pippi, then Tommy, and then Annika. The first thing they saw was a very beautiful dummy representing a fashionable lady dressed in a blue satin dress.

Pippi went up to the dummy and grasped it cordially by the hand. "How do you do, how do you do!" she said. "You are the lady who owns this store, I presume. So nice to meet you!" she continued and shook the dummy's hand even more cordially.

Then a dreadful accident happened—the dummy's arm came off and slid out of its satin sleeve, and there stood Pippi with a long white arm in her hand. Tommy gasped with terror, and Annika was beginning to cry when a clerk came rushing up to Pippi and began to scold her most dreadfully.

"Here, here, hold your horses," said Pippi after she had been listening a few minutes. "I thought this was a self-service store, and I was planning to buy this arm."

Then the clerk was angrier than ever and said that the dummy was not for sale, and in any case one couldn't sell just a single arm. But Pippi would certainly have to pay for the whole dummy because she had spoiled it.

"Well, that's very strange," said Pippi. "It's a good thing they aren't so foolish as all that in every store. Just imagine if next time I am going to have mashed turnip for dinner I go to the butcher to buy a shinbone to cook the turnip with, and he makes me take a whole pig!"

While she was speaking she casually pulled out a few gold pieces from her apron pocket and threw them down on the counter. The clerk was struck dumb with amazement.

"Does the lady cost more than that?" asked Pippi.

"No, certainly not, it doesn't cost nearly that much," said the clerk and bowed politely.

"Well, keep the change and buy something for your children," said Pippi and started toward the door. The clerk ran after her, bowing continually, and asked where she should send the dummy.

"I just want this arm and I'll take it with me," said Pippi. "The rest you can portion out among the poor. Good day!"

"But what are you going to use the arm for?" asked Tommy when they had come out on the street.

"That?" said Pippi. "What am I going to use it for? Don't people have false teeth and false hair, maybe? And even false noses sometimes? Why can't I have a little false arm? For that matter, let me tell you that it's very handy to have three arms. I remember that once when Papa and I were sailing around the world we came to a city where all the people had three arms. Wasn't that smart? Imagine, when they were sitting at the table and had a fork in one hand and a knife in the other and suddenly needed to scratch their ears—well, then it wasn't so foolish to pull out a third arm. They saved a lot of time that way, let me tell you."

Pippi looked thoughtful. "Oh, dear, now I'm lying again," she said. "It's funny, but every now and then so many lies come bubbling up inside me that I just can't help it. To tell the truth, they didn't have three arms at all in that city. They had only two."

She was silent for a minute, thinking.

"For that matter, a whole lot of them had only one arm. Well, if the truth were known, there were even some who didn't have any, and when they were going to eat they had to lie right down on their plates and lap. Scratch themselves on the ear—that they couldn't do at all; they had to ask their mothers to! That's the way it really was."

Pippi shook her head sadly. "The fact is, I've never seen a place where they had so few arms as they did in that city. But that's just like me—always trying to make myself important and wonderful and pretend that people have more arms than they have."

Pippi walked on with her false arm slung jauntily over one shoulder. She stopped in front of a candy shop. A whole row of children was standing there, gazing in at the wonderful things in the window. There were large jars full of red and blue and green candies, long rows of cakes of chocolate, mounds of chewing gum, and the most tempting lollipops. Yes, it was no wonder that the little children who stood there looking in the window now and then gave a deep sigh, for they had no money, not even the tiniest penny.

"Pippi, are we going into that store?" asked Tommy eagerly, tugging at Pippi's dress.

"That store we are going into," said Pippi, "far in!"

And in they went.

"Please, may I have thirty-six pounds of candy," said Pippi, waving a gold piece.

The clerk in the store merely stared, open-mouthed. She wasn't used to having anyone buy so much candy at once. "You mean you want thirty-six candies?" she said.

"I mean that I want thirty-six *pounds* of candy," said Pippi and put the gold piece on the counter. And then the clerk had to hurry and measure out candy in big bags. Tommy and Annika pointed out the kinds that were best. There were some red candies that were wonderful. When you had sucked them for a while you came suddenly to a wonderful creamy center. Then there were some sour green ones that weren't so bad either. Jellied raspberries and licorice boats were good too.

"We'll take six pounds of each," suggested Annika, and that is what they did.

"Then if I could have sixty lollipops and seventy-two packages of caramels, I don't think I'll need any more today except one hundred and three chocolate cigarettes," said Pippi. "There really ought to be a little cart somewhere in which I could put all this."

The clerk told Pippi she could no doubt buy a cart in the toy store next door.

Meanwhile a large crowd of children had gathered outside the candy store. They stood looking in the window and nearly fainted with excitement when they saw the scale on which Pippi did her shopping.

Pippi ran into the toy shop next door, bought a cart, and loaded all her bags on it. She looked around. Then she cried, "If there are any children here who don't eat candy, will they kindly step forward?"

Nobody stepped forward.

"Very strange," said Pippi. "Well, then, is there any child here who does eat candy?"

Twenty-three children stepped forward, and among them were, of course, Tommy and Annika.

"Tommy, open the bags," said Pippi.

Tommy did. And then began a candy-eating party the like of which had never been seen in the little town. All the children stuffed their mouths full of candies—the red ones with the delicious creamy centers, the sour green ones, the licorice boats, and the jellied raspberries. And a chocolate cigarette you could always keep in the corner of your mouth, because the chocolate flavor and the jelled-raspery flavor were terrifically good together.

From all directions children came running, and Pippi dealt out candy by the handful. "I think I'll have to go and buy thirty-six more pounds," she said, "or we shan't have any left for tomorrow."

She bought thirty-six pounds more, and there wasn't much left for tomorrow anyway.

"Now we'll go to the next store," said Pippi and stepped into the toy shop. All the children followed her. In the toy shop were all sorts of delightful things—railroad trains and automobiles you could wind up, sweet little dolls in pretty dresses, dolls' dinner sets, cap pistols and tin soldiers, and dogs and elephants made out of cloth, and bookmarks and jumping jacks.

"What can I do for you?" asked the clerk.

"We'd like a little of everything," answered Pippi, looking searchingly around the shelves. "We are very short of jumping jacks, for example," she continued, "and of cap pistols, but you can remedy that, I hope."

Pippi pulled out a fistful of gold pieces, and the children were allowed to pick out whatever they thought they most needed. Annika decided on a wonderful doll with light curly hair and a pink satin dress. It could say "Mama" when you pressed it on the stomach. Tommy wanted a popgun and a steam engine—and he got them. All the other children pointed out what they wanted too, and when Pippi had finished her shopping there wasn't very much left in the store—only a few bookmarks and building blocks. Pippi didn't buy a single thing for herself, but Mr. Nilsson got a mirror.

Just before they went out, Pippi bought each child a cuckoo whistle, and when the children got out on the street they all played on their cuckoo whistles, and Pippi beat time with her false arm. One little boy complained that his cuckoo whistle wouldn't blow. Pippi took the whistle and examined it.

"No wonder, when there's a big wad of gum in front of the hole. Where did you get hold of this treasure?" she asked and threw away a big white chunk. "As far as I know, I haven't bought any gum."

"I've had it since Friday," said the boy.

"And you aren't worried that your windpipe will grow together? I thought that was the usual end to gum-chewers."

She handed the whistle to the boy, who now could blow as merrily as all the others. There was such a racket on Main Street that at last a policeman came to see what it was all about.

"What's all this noise?" he cried.

"It is the Dress Parade March of Kronoberg's Regiment," said Pippi, "but I am not sure that all the kids realize that. Some of them seem to think we are playing 'Let your song resound like thunder!'"

(This is a famous Swedish song which begins, "Thunder like the thunder, brothers!" Only in Swedish the verb for "thunder" and the noun for "thunder" are different words.)

"Stop, this minute!" roared the policeman and held his hands over his ears.

Pippi patted his back comfortingly with her false arm. "Be thankful we didn't buy bassoons," she said.

Gradually the cuckoo whistles were silenced, one after another, until at last it was only from Tommy's whistle that there was a little peep now and then.

The policeman said emphatically that crowds were not to gather on Main Street, and all the children must go home. The children really didn't object to this at all; they wanted very much to try their new toy trains and play with their automobiles a little and put their new dolls to bed. So they all went home, happy and contented. Not one of them ate any supper that night.

Pippi and Tommy and Annika also started for home, Pippi drawing the little cart after her. She looked at all the advertisements they went by and spelled them out as well as she could.

"D-R-U-G S-T-O-R-E. Isn't that where you buy meduseen?"

"Yes, that's where you buy med-i-cine," said Annika.

"Oh, then I must go right in and buy some," said Pippi.

"Yes, but you aren't sick, are you?" said Tommy.

"What one isn't one may become," said Pippi. "There are millions of people who get sick and die just because they don't buy meduseen in time. And you are mistaken if you think such a thing is going to happen to me."

In the drug store stood the druggist, filling capsules; he was planning to fill only a few more because it was almost closing time. Then Pippi and Tommy and Annika stepped up to the counter.

"I should like to buy eight quarts of meduseen," said Pippi.

"What kind of medicine?" asked the druggist impatiently.

"Preferably some that is good for sickness," said Pippi.

"What kind of sickness?" said the druggist still more impatiently.

"Oh, let's have one that's good for whooping cough and blistered heels and belly ache and a charley horse and if you've happened to push a bean up your nose and a few little things like that. And it would be good if it was possible to polish furniture with it too. It must be really good meduseen."

The druggist said there was no medicine that was as good as all that. He claimed that different kinds of sicknesses required different kinds of medicine, and when Pippi had mentioned about ten other troubles that she wanted to cure, he put a whole row of bottles on the counter. On some of them he wrote "For External Use Only." That meant that the medicine in those bottles should only be rubbed on, and not drunk.

Pippi paid, took her bottles, thanked him, and left. Tommy and Annika followed her. The druggist looked at the clock and realized that it was closing time. He locked the door carefully and thought how good it would be to get home and have a bite to eat.

Pippi put her bottles down outside the door. "Oh, I almost forgot the most important thing of all," she said.

As the door was now locked, she put her finger on the bell and pushed long and hard. Tommy and Annika could hear how clearly it sounded inside the drug store.

After a while a little window in the door opened —it was the window where you could buy medicine if you happened to be taken ill in the night. The druggist stuck his head out. His face was quite red. "What do you want now?" he asked Pippi angrily.

"Oh, dear sir, please excuse me," said Pippi, "but I just happened to think of something. Sir, you understand sickness so well; which is better when you have a stomach-ache—to eat a hot pancake or to put your whole stomach to soak in cold water?"

The druggist's face grew redder still. "Get out," he screamed, "and be quick about it, or else—" He slammed the window.

"Gee, what a temper he's got," said Pippi. "You'd certainly think I'd done something."

She rang the bell once more, and in a few seconds the druggist's head appeared in the window again. His face was dreadfully red now.

"Pancake really is a little hard to digest, isn't it?" said Pippi and looked up at him with her friendly eyes. The druggist did not answer but shut the window again with a bang.

Pippi shrugged her shoulders. "Oh, well," she said. "I'll try warm pancake anyway. He'll have only himself to blame if anything goes wrong."

She calmly sat down on the step in front of the drug store and lined up her bottles. "How impractical grownups can be!" she said. "Here I have— let me see—eight bottles, and everything could perfectly well have gone into this one that's more than half empty anyway. It's lucky I have a little common sense myself."

With these words she pulled the corks out of the bottles and poured all the medicine into one bottle. She shook it vigorously, lifted the bottle to her mouth, and drank two good swallows.

Annika, who knew that some of the medicine was to be used only to rub on, was a little worried. "But, Pippi," she said, "how do you know that some of that medicine isn't poison?"

"I'll find out," said Pippi happily. "I'll find out by tomorrow at the latest. If I'm still alive, then we'll know that it isn't poison and the smallest child can drink it."

Tommy and Annika thought this over. After a while Tommy said doubtfully in a rather frightened voice, "Yes, but what if it is poison? Then what?"

"Then you can have what's left in the bottle to polish the dining-room furniture with," said Pippi. "Poison or not, this meduseen was not bought in vain."

She took the bottle and put it in the cart, along with the false arm, Tommy's steam engine and popgun, and Annika's doll and a bag with five little red candies in it—that was all that was left of the seventy-two pounds. Mr. Nilsson was in the cart too. He was tired and wanted to ride.

"For that matter, let me tell you that I think it is very good meduseen. I feel much better already. I feel especially healthy and happy in my tail," said Pippi, and she swung her little backside back and forth. Then off she went with the cart, home to Villa Villekulla. Tommy and Annika walked beside her and felt as if they had just a little stomach-ache.

3
Pippi Writes a Letter and Goes to School — But Only a Little Bit

"Today," said Tommy, "Annika and I wrote a letter to our grandmother."

"Did you?" said Pippi, stirring something in a kettle with the handle of her umbrella. "This is going to be a wonderful dinner," she continued, putting her nose down for a good smell. "Boil one hour, stirring vigorously, and serve immediately without ginger. What was it you said—that you wrote to your grandmother?"

"Yes," answered Tommy, who was sitting, dangling his legs, on Pippi's woodbox, "and pretty soon we'll be sure to have an answer from her."

"I never get any letters," complained Pippi.

"But you never write any either," said Annika. "You can't expect to get any unless you write some yourself."

"And that's just because you won't go to school,"

said Tommy. "You can't ever learn to write if you don't go to school."

"I can too write," said Pippi. "I know a whole lot of letters. Fridolf, who was a sailor on my father's ship, taught me a great many letters. And if I run out of letters I can always fall back on the numbers. Yes sirree, I certainly can write, but I don't know what to write about. What do you usually say in letters?"

"Oh," said Tommy, "first I usually ask Grandmother how she is, and then I tell her I'm feeling well, and then I usually talk a little about the weather and things like that. Today I also told her that I had killed a big rat in our cellar."

Pippi stirred and considered. "It's a shame that I never get any letters. All the other children get them. This state of affairs can't go on. And since I haven't any grandmother to write to me, I can write to myself. I'll do it at once."

She opened the oven door and looked in. "There ought to be a pencil in here, if I remember correctly."

There was a pencil. Pippi took it out. Then she tore in two a big white paper bag and sat down by the kitchen table. She frowned deeply, chewing on the end of her pencil.

"Don't disturb me! I'm thinking," she said.

Tommy and Annika decided to play with Mr. Nilsson while Pippi was writing. They took turns dressing and undressing him. Annika also tried to put him into the little green doll's bed where he slept. She wanted to play nurse; Tommy was to be the doctor and Mr. Nilsson the sick child. But Mr. Nilsson didn't want to lie still. He persisted in getting out of bed and hopping up and hanging by his tail from the overhead light.

Pippi raised her eyes from her writing. "Stupid Mr. Nilsson!" she said. "Sick children don't hang by the tail from the lights in the ceiling. At least not in this country. I've heard it said that they do in South Africa. There they hang a kid up on the overhead light as soon as he gets a little fever and let him hang there until he gets well again. But we aren't in South Africa now; you ought to realize that."

At last Tommy and Annika left Mr. Nilsson and went out to curry the horse. The horse was very happy when they came out on the porch. He nosed around in their hands to see if they had brought him any sugar. They hadn't, but Annika ran right back into the house and got a couple of pieces.

Pippi wrote and wrote. At last the letter was

ready. She didn't have any envelopes, but Tommy ran home for one for her. He gave her a stamp too. Pippi printed her name carefully on the envelope. "Miss Pippilotta Longstocking, Villa Villekulla."

"What does it say in the letter?" asked Annika.

"How do I know?" said Pippi. "I haven't received it yet."

Just then the mailman came by Villa Villekulla.

"Well, sometimes one does have good luck," exclaimed Pippi, "and meets a mailman just when one needs him!"

She ran out onto the street. "Will you please be so kind as to deliver this to Miss Pippi Longstocking at once?" she said. "It's urgent."

The mailman looked first at the letter and then at Pippi. "Aren't you Pippi Longstocking yourself?" he asked.

"Sure. Who did you think I was, the Empress of Abyssinia?"

"But why don't you take the letter yourself?"

"Why don't I take the letter myself?" said Pippi. "Should I be delivering the letter myself? No, that's going too far. Do you mean to say that people have to deliver their letters themselves nowadays? What do we have mailmen for, then? We might as well get rid of them. I've never in my life heard anything so foolish. No, my lad, if that's the way you do your work, they'll never make a postmaster out of you, you can be sure of that."

The mailman decided it was just as well to do what she wished, so he dropped the letter in the mailbox at Villa Villekulla. It had scarcely landed before Pippi eagerly pulled it out again.

"Oh, how curious I am!" she said to Tommy and Annika. "This is the first letter I ever got in my life."

All three children sat down on the porch steps, and Pippi slit open the envelope. Tommy and Annika looked over her shoulder and read.

DARLING PIPPI,

I SIRTINLEE HOP U R NOT SIK. IT WOOD BE 2 BAD 4 U 2 BE SIK. MYSELF I AM JUST FIN. THER IS O RONG WTH THE WETHER ETHER. YESTERDAY TOMY KILT I BIG RAT. YES.

THAT IS WHAT HE DID.

BEST WISHIS FORM

PIPPI

"Oh," said Pippi, delighted, "it says exactly the same things in my letter that it does in the one you wrote to your grandmother, Tommy. So you can be sure it is a real letter. I'll keep it as long as I live."

She put the letter in the envelope and the envelope in one of the little drawers in the big chest in the parlor. Tommy and Annika thought it was almost more fun than anything to be allowed to look at all the treasures in Pippi's chest. Every now and then Pippi would give them a little present from the chest, and still the drawers were never empty.

"Anyway," said Tommy when Pippi had put away the letter, "there were an awful lot of words spelled wrong in it."

"Yes, you really ought to go to school and learn to write a little better," said Annika.

"Thank you," said Pippi. "I went once for a whole day, and I got so much learning that it's still plopping around in my head."

"But we're going to have a picnic someday soon," said Annika. "The whole class."

"Alas!" said Pippi, biting one of her braids. "Alas! And of course I can't come just because I don't go to school. Seems as if people think they can treat you just any way if you haven't been to school and learned pluttification."

"Multiplication," said Annika emphatically.

"Yes, isn't that what I said?—'pluttification.' "

"We're going to walk about seven miles—way, way out into the woods. And then we're going to play there," said Tommy.

"Alas," said Pippi once again.

The next day was so warm and beautiful that all the school children in the little town found it very hard to sit still in their seats. The teacher opened all the windows and let the sun come streaming in. Just outside the school window stood a birch tree, and high up in it sat a little starling, singing so cheerily that the children just listened to him and didn't care at all that nine times nine equals eighty-one.

Suddenly Tommy jumped up in amazement. "Look, Teacher," he cried, pointing out of the window, "there's Pippi!" All the children turned to look and, sure enough, there sat Pippi on a branch of the birch tree. She was sitting very close to the window, for the branch reached almost down to the window sill.

"Hi, Teacher!" she cried. "Hi, kids!"

"Good morning, little Pippi," said the teacher. Once Pippi had come to school for a whole day, so the teacher knew her very well. Pippi and the teacher had agreed that Pippi might come back to school when she grew a little older and more sensible.

"What do you want, little Pippi?" asked the teacher.

"Oh, I was just going to ask you to throw a little

pluttification out of the window," said Pippi, "as much as would be necessary for me to be allowed to go to the picnic with you. And if you have discovered any new letters, you might throw them out at the same time."

"Don't you want to come in for a little while?" asked the teacher.

"I'd rather not," said Pippi honestly, leaning back comfortably on the branch. "I just get dizzy. The knowledge in there is so thick you can cut it with a knife. But don't you think, Teacher," she continued hopefully, "that a little of that knowledge might fly out through the window and stick to me —just enough so that I could go with you on the picnic?"

"It might," said the teacher, and then went on with the arithmetic lesson. All the children thought it was very pleasant to have Pippi sitting in a tree outside. She had given them all candy and toys that day when she went shopping. Pippi had Mr. Nilsson with her, of course, and the children thought it was fun to see how he threw himself from one branch to another. Sometimes he even hopped down into the window, and once he took a long jump and landed right on Tommy's head and began to scratch his hair. But then the teacher told Pippi she'd have to call Mr. Nilsson because Tommy was just going to figure out how much 315 divided by 7 is, and you can't do that when you have a monkey in your hair. But anyway, lessons just wouldn't go right that morning. The spring sunshine, the starling, and Pippi and Mr. Nilsson—all this was just too much for the children.

"I don't know what's got into you, children," said the teacher.

"Do you know what, Teacher?" said Pippi out in the tree. "To tell the truth, I don't think this is the right kind of a day for pluttification."

"We're doing division," said the teacher.

"On this kind of day you shouldn't have any kind of 'shun,'" said Pippi, "unless of course it's recreation."

Teacher gave up. "Maybe you can furnish some recreation, Pippi," she said.

"No, I'm not very good at recreation," said Pippi, suddenly hanging over the branch by her knee joints so that her red braids almost touched the ground. "But I know a school where they don't have anything but recreation. 'All Day: Recreation' is what it says on the school program."

"Is that so?" said the teacher. "And where is that school?"

"In Australia," said Pippi. "In a little village in Australia. Way down in the southern part." She sat up on the branch again, and her eyes began to sparkle.

"What kind of recreation do they have?" asked the teacher.

"Oh, all kinds," said Pippi. "Usually they begin by jumping out of the window, one after another. Then they give a terrific yell and rush into the schoolroom again and skip around on the seats as fast as ever they can."

"But what does their teacher say then?" asked the teacher.

"She?" said Pippi. "Oh, she skips too—faster than anyone else. Then the children usually fight for half an hour or so, and the teacher stands near and cheers them on. When the weather is rainy all the kids take off their clothes and rush out into the rain and dance and jump. The teacher plays a march on the organ for them so that they can keep time. Some of them stand under the rainspout so that they can have a real shower."

"Do they indeed?" said the teacher.

"They certainly do," said Pippi, "and it's an awfully good school, one of the better ones in Australia. But it is very far down in the south."

"Yes, I can imagine so," said the teacher. "But I don't think we'll have as much fun as all that in this school."

"Too bad," said Pippi. "If it was only a matter of skipping around on the seats I'd dare to come in for a while."

"You'll have to wait to skip until we have the picnic," said the teacher.

"Oh, may I really go to the picnic?" cried Pippi, and was so happy that she turned a somersault backward right out of the tree. "I'll certainly write and tell them about that in Australia. Then they can keep on with their recreation as much as they want to. Because a picnic is certainly more fun."

4
Pippi Goes to the School Picnic

There was a tramping of many feet on the ground, and much talk and laughter. There was Tommy with a knapsack on his back, and Annika in a brand-new cotton dress, and their teacher and all their classmates except one poor child who had the misfortune to get a sore throat on the very day of the picnic. And there in front of all the others was Pippi, riding on her horse. Back of her sat Mr. Nilsson with his pocket mirror in his hand. Yes, there he sat, catching the sun's light in the mirror and looking extraordinarily pleased when he managed to reflect it right in Tommy's eye.

Annika had been absolutely sure it would rain on this important day. In fact, she had been so sure of it that she had almost been angry at the weather in advance. But just think how lucky you can be sometimes—the sun continued to shine just as usual, even if it was picnic day, and Annika's heart almost jumped for joy as she walked along the road in her brand-new cotton dress. For that matter, all the children looked happy and eager. Pussy willows were growing everywhere along the roadside, and in one place there was a whole field of wild flowers. All the children decided to pick big bunches of pussy willows and bouquets of yellow wild flowers on the way home.

"Such a glorious, glorious day," said Annika with a sigh, looking up at Pippi, who sat on her horse as straight as a general.

"Yes, I haven't had so much fun since I fought with the champion boxer in San Francisco," said Pippi. "Would you like to ride a little while?"

Annika would indeed, so Pippi lifted her up onto the horse's back, and there she rode, right in front of Pippi. When the other children saw her, of course they all wanted to ride too. And Pippi let them, each in turn. But Tommy and Annika were allowed to ride a little longer than most of the others. There was one girl who had a blister on her heel. She was allowed to sit behind Pippi and ride all the way. Mr. Nilsson pulled her braids whenever he could get hold of them.

The picnic was to be held in a wood which was called the Monsters' Forest—probably, Pippi thought, because it was so monstrously beautiful.

When they were almost there Pippi jumped out of the saddle, patted her horse, and said, "Now you've carried us for such a long time that you must be tired. It isn't right for one person to do all the work."

And she lifted the horse up in her strong arms and carried him until they came to a little clearing in the woods and the teacher said, "We'll stop here."

Pippi looked around and screamed, "Come out now, all you monsters, and let's see who is the strongest."

The teacher explained that there were no monsters in the woods, and Pippi was much disappointed.

"A Forest of Monsters without any monsters! What will folks think of next? Soon they'll invent fires without any fire and a Christmas-tree gift party without any Christmas tree—just out of stinginess. But on the day they begin having candy stores without any candy, I'll go and tell them a thing or two. Oh, well, I'll have to be a monster myself, I suppose. I don't see any other way out of it."

She let out such a terrific roar that the teacher had to hold her hands over her ears, and several of the children were scared almost to death.

"Oh, yes, we'll play that Pippi is a monster," cried Tommy, enchanted, and clapped his hands.

All the children thought that was a fine idea. The Monster then went into a deep crevice between the rocks, which was to be its den, and all the children ran around outside, teasing and yelling, "Stupid, stupid Monster! Stupid, stupid Monster!"

Out rushed the Monster, bellowing and chasing the children, who ran in all directions to hide. Those who were captured were dragged home to the den in the rocks, and the Monster said they were to be cooked for dinner. Sometimes they managed to escape while the Monster was out hunting for more children, although in order to get away they had to climb up a steep rock and that was hard work. There was only one little pine tree to get hold of, and it was difficult to know where to put one's feet. But it was very exciting, and the children thought it was the best game they had ever played.

The teacher lay in the green grass, reading a book and casting a glance at the children every now and then. "That's the wildest monster I ever saw," she mumbled to herself.

And it certainly was. The Monster jumped around and bellowed and threw three or four boys over its shoulder at once and dragged them down into the den. Sometimes the Monster climbed furiously up into the highest treetops and skipped from branch to branch, just as if it were a monkey. Sometimes it threw itself upon the horse's back and chased a whole crowd of children who were trying to escape through the trees. With the horse still in full gallop, the Monster would lean down from the saddle, snatch up the children, place them in front of itself on the horse, and gallop madly back to the den, yelling, "Now I'm going to cook you for dinner!"

It was such fun the children thought they'd never want to stop. But suddenly everything was quiet, and when Tommy and Annika came running to see what was the matter they found the Monster sitting on a stone with a very strange expression on its face, looking at something in its hand.

"He's dead. Look, he's absolutely dead," said the Monster.

It was a little baby bird that was dead. It had fallen out of the nest and killed itself.

"Oh, what a shame!" said Annika. The Monster nodded.

"Pippi, you're crying," said Tommy suddenly.

"Crying? Me?" said Pippi. "Of course I'm not crying."

"Yes, but your eyes are all red," insisted Tommy.

"My eyes red?" said Pippi, and borrowed Mr. Nilsson's pocket mirror to see. "Do you call that red? Then you ought to have been with Father and me in Batavia. There was a man there whose eyes were so red that the police refused to allow him on the streets."

"Why?" asked Tommy.

"Because people thought he was a stop sign, of course. And there was a dreadful traffic jam every time he came out. Red eyes? Me? No sirree, you needn't think I'd cry for a little scrap of a bird like this," said Pippi.

"Stupid, stupid Monster! Stupid, stupid Monster!" From all directions the children came running to see where the Monster was hiding. The Monster took the little scrap of a bird and laid it down very carefully on a bed of soft moss.

"If I could, I'd bring you to life again," she said with a deep sigh.

Then she let out a terrific yell. "Now I'll cook you for dinner," she shrieked. And with happy shouts the children disappeared into the bushes.

One of the girls in the class—her name was Ulla—lived right near the Forest of Monsters. Ulla's mother had promised her that she could invite her teacher and her classmates—and Pippi, too, of course—for refreshments in the garden. So when the children had played the monster game for a long time, and climbed about among the rocks for a while, and sailed their birch-bark boats on a large pool, and seen how many of them dared to jump off a high stone, then Ulla said that it must be time to go to her house to have their fruit punch. And the teacher, who had read her book from cover to cover, agreed. She gathered the children together and they left the Forest of the Monsters.

Out on the road they met a man with a wagon-load of sacks. They were heavy sacks and there were many of them, and the man's horse was tired. All of a sudden one of the wagon wheels went down into the ditch. The man, whose name was Mr. Blomster-lund, became terrifically angry. He thought it was the horse's fault. He got out his whip and immediately began to beat the horse fast and furiously. The horse pulled and tugged and tried with all its might to pull the load up onto the road again, but it couldn't do it. Mr. Blomsterlund grew angrier and angrier and beat harder and harder. Then the teacher noticed him and was almost overcome with sympathy for the poor horse.

"How can you bear to beat an animal that way?" she said to Mr. Blomsterlund.

He let the whip rest a moment and spat before he answered. "Don't interfere with what doesn't concern you," said he. "Otherwise it might just happen that I'll give you a taste of the whip too, the whole lot of you."

He spat once more and picked up the whip again. The poor horse trembled through its whole body.

Then something came dashing through the crowd of children like a flash of lightning. It was Pippi. She was absolutely white around the nose, and when Pippi was white around the nose she was *angry.* Tommy and Annika knew that. She rushed at Mr. Blomsterlund, caught him around the waist, and threw him high up in the air. When he came down, she caught him and threw him up again. Four, five, six times he had to take a trip up into the air. He didn't know what had happened to him.

"Help! Help!" he cried, terrified. At last he landed with a thump on the road. He had lost the whip.

Pippi went and stood in front of him with her hands on her hips. "You are not to hit that horse any more. You are not to do it, I tell you. Once down in Cape Town I met another man who was whipping his horse. He had on such a beautiful uniform, that man, and I told him that if he ever whipped his horse again I'd scratch and claw him so that there wouldn't be one single thread left whole in his beautiful uniform. Just imagine, a week later he did whip his horse again. Wasn't it too bad about such a nice uniform?"

Mr. Blomsterlund was still sitting in the road, completely bewildered.

"Where are you going with your load?" asked Pippi.

Mr. Blomsterlund, still frightened, pointed at a

cottage a little way down the road. "Home, over there," he said.

Then Pippi unhitched the horse, which stood there trembling with weariness and fright. "There, there, little horsie!" she said. "Now you'll see another kettle of fish!"

With that she lifted it up in her strong arms and carried it home to its stall. The horse looked just as astonished as Mr. Blomsterlund did.

All the children were standing with the teacher, waiting for Pippi. And Mr. Blomsterlund stood by his load, scratching his head. He didn't know how he was going to get it home.

Then Pippi came back. She took one of the big, heavy sacks and hung it on Mr. Blomsterlund's back.

"There now!" she said. "Let's see if you're as good at carrying as you were at whipping." She picked up the whip. "I really ought to give you a few whacks with this since you seem to be so fond of whippings. But the whip is beginning to wear out," she added and broke off a piece of it. "Completely worn out, sad to say," she continued, and broke the whole whip into tiny, tiny pieces.

Mr. Blomsterlund with his sack was trudging along the road without saying a word. He only puffed a little. And Pippi took hold of the wagon shafts and pulled the wagon home for him.

"There, that won't cost you a cent," she said when she had deposited the wagon outside Mr. Blomsterlund's barn. "I was glad to do it. The trips up into the air were free too."

Then she went away. Mr. Blomsterlund stood staring after her for a long time.

"Three cheers for Pippi," cried the children when she came back.

The teacher too was much pleased with Pippi and praised her. "That was well done," said she. "We should always be kind to animals—and to people too, of course."

Pippi sat on her horse, looking perfectly satisfied. "Well, I certainly was good to Mr. Blomsterlund, anyway," she said. "All that flying in the air for nothing!"

"That is why we are here," said the teacher, "to be good and kind to other people."

Pippi stood on her head on the horse's back and waved her legs in the air. "Heigh-ho," said she, "then why are the other people here?"

A large table had been set in Ulla's garden. There were so many buns and cakes on it that they made the children's mouths water, and they all hurried to find places at the table. Pippi sat down at one end.

The first thing she did was to snatch two buns and cram them into her mouth. She looked like a cherub with her puffed-out cheeks.

"Pippi, it is customary to wait until one is invited to have something," said the teacher reproachfully.

"Oh, you don't need to shtand on sheremony on my account," said Pippi with her mouth full. "I don't mind if everything is informal."

Just then Ulla's mother came up to Pippi. She had a pitcher of fruit punch in one hand and a pot of chocolate in the other. "Punch or chocolate?" she asked.

"Punch *and* chocolate," said Pippi. "I'll send punch after one bun and chocolate after the other." Without waiting to be urged, she took from Ulla's mother both the punch pitcher and the chocolate pot and drank a deep draught from each.

"She has been at sea all her life," the teacher explained in a whisper to Ulla's mother, who looked much astonished.

"Oh, I see." She nodded and decided to pay no attention to Pippi's bad manners. "Will you have molasses cookies?" she asked and passed the plate of them to Pippi.

"Well, it looks as if I would," said Pippi, giggling happily at her own joke. "To be sure, you didn't have very good luck cutting them out, but I hope they'll taste good anyway," she continued, taking a handful.

Suddenly she noticed some pretty pink cakes a little way down on the table. She pulled Mr. Nilsson lightly by the tail. "Look, Mr. Nilsson, skip over and get me one of those pink thingamajigs. You might as well take two or three while you're about it."

And Mr. Nilsson dashed away, right across the table so that the punch glasses splashed over.

"I hope you have had enough?" asked Ulla's mother when Pippi came up to say thank you after the party.

"No, I haven't. I'm thirsty," said Pippi, scratching her ear.

"Well, we didn't have so very much to treat you on," said Ulla's mother.

"No, but at least you had something," said Pippi pleasantly.

After this, the teacher decided to have a little talk with Pippi about her behavior. "Listen, little Pippi," she said in a friendly voice, "you want to be a really fine lady when you grow up, don't you?"

"You mean the kind with a veil on her nose and three double chins under it?" asked Pippi.

"I mean a lady who always knows how to behave and is always polite and well bred. You want to be that kind of a lady, don't you?"

"It's worth thinking about," said Pippi, "but you see, Teacher, I had just about decided to be a pirate when I grow up." She thought a while. "But don't you think, Teacher, one could be a pirate and a really fine lady too? Because then—"

The teacher didn't think one could.

"Oh, dear, oh, dear, which one shall I decide on?" said Pippi unhappily.

The teacher said that whatever Pippi decided to do when she grew up, it would not hurt her to learn how to behave—because Pippi's behavior at the table was really impossible.

"To think it should be so hard to know how to behave." Pippi sighed. "Can't you tell me the most important rules?"

The teacher did the best she could, and Pippi listened attentively. One mustn't help oneself until one was invited; one mustn't take more than one cake at a time; one mustn't eat with a knife; one mustn't scratch oneself while talking with other people; one mustn't do this and one mustn't do that.

Pippi nodded thoughtfully. "I'll get up an hour earlier every morning and practice," she said, "so I'll get the hang of it in case I decide not to be a pirate."

Now the teacher said it was time to go home. All the children stood in line except Pippi. She sat still on the lawn with a tense face, as if she were listening to something.

"What's the matter, little Pippi?" asked the teacher.

"Teacher," asked Pippi, "does a really fine lady's stomach ever rumble?"

She sat quiet, still listening.

"Because if it doesn't," she said at last, "I might just as well decide to be a pirate."

5

Pippi Goes
to the Fair

Once every year a fair was held in the little town,
and all the children were simply wild with joy that
anything so nice could happen. The town looked
quite different on Fair Day. There were big crowds
in the streets, flags were flying, and in the market-
place were booths where you could buy the most
wonderful things. There was so much commotion
that it was exciting just to walk in the streets. Best
of all, down by the city gate there was a carnival
with a merry-go-round and shooting galleries and a
tent show and all kinds of things. And there was a
menagerie—a menagerie with wild animals: tigers
and giant snakes and monkeys and trained seals!
You could stand outside the menagerie and hear
the strangest growling and roaring you ever heard
in all your life, and if you had money you could, of
course, go in and see everything too.

No wonder that even the bow in Annika's hair

trembled with excitement when she had finished dressing on the morning of the fair. Or that Tommy swallowed his cheese sandwich almost whole. Tommy's and Annika's mother asked them if they didn't want to go to the fair with her, but they squirmed and wiggled and said if she didn't mind, they would rather go with Pippi.

"For you see," explained Tommy to Annika as they ran through the garden gate at Villa Villekulla, "I think more funny things will happen where Pippi is."

Annika thought so too.

Pippi was all dressed up and standing right in the middle of the kitchen floor, waiting for them. She had at last found her big cartwheel hat in the woodshed.

"I forgot that I used it to carry wood in the other day," she said, and pulled the hat down over her eyes. "Don't I look nice?"

Tommy and Annika had to admit that she did. She had blackened her eyebrows with a piece of charcoal and had painted her lips and her nails red, and then she had put on a very fine evening dress that reached to the floor. It was cut low in the back and showed her red flannel underwear. Her big black shoes stuck out from under her skirt, and they were even finer than usual, for she had tied on them the big green rosettes she wore only on special occasions.

"I think one should look like a really fine lady when one goes to the fair," she said, and she tripped down the road as daintily as was possible in such big shoes. She lifted up the edge of her skirt and, holding it away from her, said in a voice that didn't sound at all like her own, "Chawming, chawming."

"What is it that's so charming?" asked Tommy.

"Me!" said Pippi happily.

Tommy and Annika thought that everything was charming when there was a fair in town. It was charming to mingle with the crowd and to go from one booth to another on the square and look at all the things displayed there. Pippi bought a red silk scarf for Annika as a souvenir of the fair, and for Tommy a visor cap which he had always longed for but which his mother didn't want him to have. In another booth Pippi bought two glass bells filled with pink and white candies.

"Oh, how kind you are, Pippi!" said Annika, hugging her bell.

"Oh, yes, chawming," said Pippi. "Chawming," she said, lifting her skirt gracefully.

A stream of people moved slowly down the street from the square to the carnival. Pippi, Tommy, and Annika went along.

"Gee, isn't this great!" said Tommy.

The organ grinder played, the merry-go-round went round and round, the people laughed joyously. The dart-throwing and china-breaking were in full swing. People crowded around the shooting galleries to show their skill.

"I'd like to look a little closer at that," said Pippi and pulled Tommy and Annika with her to a shooting gallery.

Just then there was no one at that particular gallery, and the lady who was supposed to be handing out guns and taking in money was cross. She didn't think three children would make very good customers, and so she paid no attention to them. Pippi looked at the target with great interest. It was a cardboard man with a round face, dressed in a blue coat. Right in the middle of his face was a red nose, which you were supposed to hit. If you couldn't hit his nose, you should at least come close to it. Shots that didn't hit his face weren't counted.

It annoyed the lady to see the children standing there. She wanted customers who could both shoot and pay.

"Are you still hanging around here?" she said angrily.

"No," said Pippi seriously, "we're sitting in the middle of the square cracking nuts."

"What are you glaring at?" asked the lady, still

more angrily. "Are you waiting for someone to come and shoot?"

"No," said Pippi, "we're waiting for you to start turning somersaults."

Just then a customer came up, a very fine gentleman with a big gold chain over his stomach. He took a gun and weighed it in his hand.

"I think I'll take a few shots just to show how it's done," he said.

He looked around to see if he had any audience, but there was no one except Pippi, Tommy, and Annika.

"Look here, children," he said. "Watch me and I'll give you your first lesson in the art of shooting."

He lifted the gun to his cheek. The first shot was way off, the second shot also; the third and fourth were still farther from the nose. The fifth shot hit the cardboard man on the bottom of his chin.

"The gun's no good!" said the fine gentleman and threw it down.

Pippi picked it up and loaded it. "My, how well you shoot!" she said. "Another time I'll shoot just as you taught us, and not like this."

Pang, pang, pang, pang, pang! Five shots had hit the cardboard man right in the middle of his nose. Pippi gave the lady a gold piece and walked off.

The merry-go-round was so marvelous that

Tommy and Annika held their breath in awe when they saw it. There were black and white and brown wooden horses to ride on. They had real manes and tails and looked almost alive. They also had saddles and reins. You could choose any horse you wanted. Pippi bought a whole gold piece's worth of tickets. She got so many there was hardly room for them in her big purse.

"If I had given them another gold coin, I think I would have got the whole whirling thingamajig," she said to Tommy and Annika, who stood waiting for her.

Tommy decided on a black horse, and Annika took a white one. Pippi placed Mr. Nilsson on a black horse that looked very wild. Mr. Nilsson immediately began to scratch the horse's mane to see if it had fleas.

"Is Mr. Nilsson going to ride the merry-go-round too?" asked Annika, surprised.

"Of course," said Pippi. "If I'd thought about it I would have brought my horse too. He really needed a bit of entertainment, and a horse who rides on a horse—that would have been really horsy."

Pippi threw herself into the saddle of a brown horse, and the next second the merry-go-round started, and the music played "Do you remember our childhood days, with all their jolly fun?"

Tommy and Annika thought it was wonderful to ride the merry-go-round, and Pippi looked as though she were enjoying herself too. She stood on her head on her horse with her legs straight up in the air. Her long evening dress fell down around her neck. The people who were watching saw only a red flannel shirt and a pair of green pants, Pippi's long, thin legs with one black and one brown stocking, and her large black shoes playfully waving back and forth.

"That's the way a really fine lady rides the merry-go-round!" exclaimed Pippi at the end of the first ride.

The children rode the merry-go-round a whole hour, but at last Pippi was dizzy and said that she saw three merry-go-rounds instead of one.

"It's so hard to decide which one to ride on," she said, "so I think we'll go some other place."

She had a whole lot of tickets left, and these she gave to some little children who hadn't ridden at all because they didn't have any money for tickets.

Outside a tent nearby, a man was shouting, "New show starts in five minutes. Don't miss this wonderful opportunity to see 'The Murder of the Countess Aurora' or 'Who's Sneaking Around in the Bushes?' Right this way, folks, right this way for the big show!"

"If there's someone sneaking around in the bushes we'll have to go in and find out who it is, and immediately!" said Pippi to Tommy and Annika. "Come on, let's go in!"

She walked up to the ticket window. "Can't I go in for half price if I promise to look with just one eye?" she asked with a sudden attack of economy.

But the ticket seller wouldn't hear of anything like that.

"I don't see any bushes, and no one to sneak around in them either," said Pippi disgustedly when she and Tommy and Annika had seated themselves on the front bench.

"It hasn't started yet," said Tommy.

Just then the curtain went up, and the Countess Aurora was seen walking back and forth on the stage. She wrung her hands and looked worried. Pippi followed every move with breathless interest.

"She must feel sad," she said to Tommy and Annika, "or maybe she has a safety pin that is sticking her some place."

Countess Aurora *was* feeling sad. She raised her eyes to the ceiling and said in a plaintive voice, "Is there anyone as unhappy as I? My children taken away from me, my husband disappeared, and I myself surrounded by villains and bandits who want to kill me."

"Oh, how terrible it is to hear this," said Pippi, whose eyes were getting red.

"I wish I were dead already," said the Countess Aurora.

Pippi burst out crying. "Please don't talk like that!" She sniffed. "Things will be brighter for you. The children will find their way home, and you can always get another husband. There are so many me-e-en," she gasped between her sobs.

The manager of the show—the one who had stood outside—came up to Pippi and told her that if she didn't keep absolutely quiet she would have to leave the theater at once.

"I'll try," said Pippi, wiping her eyes.

The play was terribly exciting. Tommy sat through it all twisting and turning his cap from sheer nervousness. Annika held her hands tightly clasped in her lap. Pippi's bright eyes didn't leave Countess Aurora a minute.

Things were growing worse and worse for the poor countess. She walked in the palace garden, suspecting nothing. Suddenly there was a loud cry. It was Pippi. She had seen a man hiding behind a tree, and he didn't look like a kind man.

Countess Aurora must have heard something rustling, for she said in a frightened voice, "Who's sneaking around in the bushes?"

"I can tell you!" said Pippi excitedly. "It's a horrible man with a black mustache. Run into the woodshed and lock the door, quick!"

The manager came up to Pippi and said she would have to leave at once.

"And leave the Countess Aurora alone with that horrid man! You don't know me, mister," answered Pippi.

On the stage the play went on. Suddenly the "horrid man" sprang from the bushes and threw himself at the Countess Aurora.

"Ha! Your last hour has come," he hissed.

"Oh, it has, has it?" cried Pippi. "We'll see about that!" And with one jump she was on the stage. Grabbing the villain around the waist, she threw him across the footlights onto the floor of the auditorium. She was still crying.

"How can you?" she sobbed. "What have you against the countess anyway? Remember that her children and her husband have left her and she's all alo-o-one."

She went up to the countess, who had sunk down on the garden seat, completely exhausted.

"You can come and live with me in Villa Ville-kulla if you want to," Pippi said comfortingly.

Sobbing loudly, Pippi stumbled out of the theater, followed by Tommy and Annika—and the manager. He shook his fist after Pippi, but the people in the audience clapped their hands and thought she had given a good performance.

Outside, Pippi blew her nose and, quickly regaining her composure, said, "Come, we'll have to cheer up. This was too sad."

"The menagerie," said Tommy. "We haven't been to the menagerie."

On their way to the menagerie they stopped at a sandwich stand, and Pippi bought six sandwiches for each of them and three big bottles of soda.

"Crying always makes me so hungry," explained Pippi.

There were many things to see inside the menagerie—an elephant and two tigers in a cage, and several large trained seals that were throwing a ball to one another, and a whole lot of monkeys and a hyena and two giant snakes. Pippi took Mr. Nilsson over to the monkey cage so that he could speak to his relatives. An old chimpanzee sat there, looking very sad.

"Come on, Mr. Nilsson," said Pippi, "speak up

nicely now. I imagine this is your grandfather's cousin's aunt's mother-in-law's nephew."

Mr. Nilsson doffed his straw hat and spoke as politely as he knew how, but the chimpanzee didn't bother to answer.

The two giant snakes lay in a big box. Every hour the beautiful snake charmer, Mademoiselle Paula, took them from their box and did an act with them on the stage. The children were lucky, for they came in just in time for the performance. Annika was so afraid of snakes that she held tightly to Pippi's arm.

Mademoiselle Paula lifted one of the snakes up —a big, ugly thing—and put it around her neck like a scarf.

"That looks like a boa constrictor," whispered Pippi to Tommy and Annika. "I wonder what kind the other one is."

She went over to the box and lifted up the other snake. It was still larger and uglier. Pippi put it around her neck just as Mademoiselle Paula had done. All the people in the menagerie cried out in horror. Mademoiselle Paula threw her snake into the box and rushed over to try to save Pippi from certain death. Pippi's snake was frightened and angry from the noise, and he couldn't at all understand why he should be hanging around the neck of a little redheaded girl instead of around Mademoiselle Paula's neck as he was used to doing. He decided to teach the little redheaded girl a lesson and contracted his body in a grip that would ordinarily choke an ox.

"Don't try that old trick on me," said Pippi. "I've seen larger snakes than you, you know, in Farthest India."

She pulled the snake away from her throat and put him back into the box. Tommy and Annika stood there, pale with fright.

"That was a boa constrictor too," said Pippi, fastening one of her garters that had come loose, "just as I thought."

Mademoiselle Paula scolded her for several minutes in some foreign language, and all the people in the menagerie drew a long breath in relief, but their relief was short-lived, for this was evidently a day when THINGS happened.

Afterward no one knew just how the next thing had happened. The tigers had been fed large red chunks of meat, and the keeper said he was sure he had locked the door of the cage, but a minute later a terrible cry was heard—"A tiger is loose!"

It was. There, outside the cage, lay the yellow striped beast, ready to spring. The people fled in all directions—all but one little girl who stood squeezed into a corner right next to the tiger.

"Stand perfectly still," the people called to her. They hoped the tiger would not touch her if she didn't move. "What shall we do?" they cried, wringing their hands.

"Run for the police!" someone suggested.

"Call the fire department!" cried another.

"Bring Pippi Longstocking!" cried Pippi, and stepped forward. She squatted a couple of yards from the tiger and called to him. "Pussy, pussy, pussy!"

The tiger growled ferociously and showed his enormous teeth. Pippi held up a warning finger. "If you bite me, I'll bite you. You can be sure of that!"

Then the tiger sprang right at her.

"What's this? Don't you understand a joke?" cried Pippi and pushed the tiger away.

With a loud snarl that made cold shivers go up and down everyone's back, the tiger threw himself at Pippi a second time. You could plainly see that he intended to bite her throat.

"So you want to fight, eh?" said Pippi. "Well, just remember that it was you who started it."

With one hand she pressed together the huge jaws of the tiger, picked him up, and, cradling him in her arms, tenderly carried him back to the cage,

singing a little song. "Have you seen my little pussy, little pussy, little pussy?"

The people drew a sigh of relief for a second time, and the little girl who had stood squeezed into the corner ran to her mother and said she never wanted to go to a menagerie again.

The tiger had torn the hem of Pippi's dress. Pippi looked at the rags and said, "Does anyone have a pair of scissors?"

Mademoiselle Paula had a pair, and she wasn't angry with Pippi any more.

"Here you are, you brave little girl," she said and gave Pippi the scissors.

Pippi cut her dress off a few inches above the knees.

"There!" she said happily. "Now I'm finer than ever. My dress is cut low at the neck and high at the knees; you really couldn't find a finer dress."

She tripped off so elegantly that her knees hit each other at each step. "Chawming!" she said.

You would have thought that there had been enough excitement for one day at the fair, but fairs are never very quiet places, and it was soon evident that the people had again drawn their breath in relief too soon.

In the little town lived a very bad man—a very

strong bad man. All the children were afraid of him —and not only the children but everyone else too. Even the policemen preferred to stay out of the way when the bad man, Laban, was on the warpath.

He wasn't angry all the time, only when he had drunk ale, and he had had quite a bit of ale the day of the fair. Yelling and bellowing, he came down Main Street, swinging his huge arms.

"Out of the way," he cried, "for here comes Laban!"

The people anxiously backed up against the walls, and many children cried in terror. There was no policeman in sight. Laban made his way toward the carnival. He was terrible to look at with his long black hair hanging down over his forehead, his big red nose, and one yellow tooth sticking out of his mouth. The crowd at the carnival thought that he looked even more ferocious than the tiger.

A little old man stood in a booth, selling hot dogs. Laban went up to the booth, struck his fist on the counter, and yelled, "Give me a hot dog and be quick about it!"

The old man gave him a hot dog at once. "That will be fifty cents," he said timidly.

"Do you charge for a hot dog when you serve it

to such a fine gentleman as Laban? Aren't you ashamed of yourself? Hand over another one."

The old man said that first he must have the money for the one that Laban had already eaten. Then Laban took hold of the old man's ears and shook him.

"Hand over another hot dog," he demanded, "this instant!"

The old man didn't dare disobey, but the people who stood around couldn't help muttering disapprovingly. One was even brave enough to say, "It's disgraceful to treat a poor old man like that."

Laban turned around. He looked at the crowd with his bloodshot eyes. "Did someone sneeze?" He sneered.

The crowd sensed trouble and wanted to leave.

"Stand still!" shouted Laban. "I'll bash in the head of the first one who moves. Stand still, I say, for Laban will now give a little show."

He took a whole handful of hot dogs and began to juggle them. He threw them into the air and caught some of them in his mouth and some in his hands, but several fell on the ground. The poor old hot dog man almost cried.

Suddenly a little form darted out of the crowd. Pippi stopped right in front of Laban.

"Whose little boy can this be?" she asked sweetly.

"And what will his Mommy say when he throws his breakfast around like this?"

Laban gave a terrifying growl. "Didn't I say that everyone should stand still?" he shouted.

"Do you always turn on the loudspeaker?" wondered Pippi.

Laban raised a threatening fist and yelled, "Brat!!! Do I have to make hash out of you before you shut up?"

Pippi stood with her hands at her sides and looked at him with interest. "What was it you did to the hot dogs? Was it this?" She threw Laban high up into the air and juggled with him for a few minutes. The people cheered. The old man clapped his hands and smiled.

When Pippi had finished, a very much frightened and confused Laban sat on the ground, looking around.

"Now I think the bad man should go home," said Pippi.

Laban had no objection.

"But before you go there are some hot dogs to be paid for," said Pippi.

Laban stood up and paid for eighteen hot dogs, and then he left without a word. He was never quite himself after that day.

"Three cheers for Pippi!" cried the people.

"Hurrah for Pippi!" cried Tommy and Annika.

"We don't need a policeman in this town," somebody said, "as long as we have Pippi Longstocking."

"No, sir!" said someone else. "She takes care of both tigers and bad men."

"Of course we have to have a policeman," said Pippi. "Someone has to see to it that the bicycles stand decently parked in the wrong places."

"Oh, Pippi, you were wonderful!" said Annika as the children walked home from the fair.

"Oh, yes, chawming!" said Pippi.

She held up her skirt—which already came only halfway to her knees. "Really, most chawming!"

6
Pippi Is
Shipwrecked

Every day as soon as school was out Tommy and Annika rushed over to Villa Villekulla. They didn't even want to do their homework at their own house but took their books over to Pippi's instead.

"That's good," said Pippi. "Sit here and study, and no doubt a little knowledge will soak into me. Not that I really think I need it, but I suppose I can never be a really fine lady unless I know how many Hottentots there are in Australia."

Tommy and Annika sat at the kitchen table with their geographies in front of them. Pippi sat in the middle of the table with her legs tucked under her.

"Just think," said Pippi thoughtfully, pressing her finger on the end of her nose. "Suppose I did learn how many Hottentots there are in Australia and then one of them should go and get pneumonia and die, my count would be wrong; I would have had all that trouble for nothing, and I still wouldn't be a really fine lady."

She thought about it a few minutes. "Someone ought to tell the Hottentots to behave themselves so there wouldn't be any mistakes in your school-books."

When Tommy and Annika were through with their homework the fun began. If the weather was nice they played in the garden, rode horseback a little, or clambered up on the laundry roof and sat there drinking coffee, or climbed up into the old hollow oak tree and let themselves down into the trunk. Pippi said that it was a very remarkable tree, for soda grew in it. That seemed to be true, for every time the children climbed down into their hiding place inside the oak they found three bottles of soda waiting for them. Tommy and Annika couldn't understand what happened to the empty bottles, but Pippi said they wilted away as soon as they were emptied. Yes, it was indeed a strange tree, thought both Tommy and Annika. Sometimes chocolate bars grew there too, but Pippi said that was only on Thursdays. Tommy and Annika were very careful to go there and pick chocolate bars every Thursday. Pippi said that if you just gave yourself time to water the tree decently you could probably get

French bread to grow there too, and perhaps even a small roast of veal.

If it rained they had to stay in the house, and that wasn't bad either. They could look at all the fine things in Pippi's chest, or sit in front of the stove and watch Pippi make waffles or fry apples, or climb into the woodbox and sit there listening to Pippi telling exciting stories about the time when she sailed the seas.

"Goodness, how it stormed!" Pippi would say. "Even the fishes were seasick and wanted to go ashore. I saw a shark that was absolutely green in the face and an octopus that sat holding his head in all his many arms. My, my, what a storm that was!"

"Oh, weren't you afraid, Pippi?" asked Annika.

"Yes, just suppose you had been shipwrecked!" said Tommy.

"Oh, well," said Pippi, "I've been more or less shipwrecked so many times that I wasn't exactly afraid —not at first, anyway. I wasn't afraid when the raisins blew out of the fruit soup at dinner, and not when the cook's false teeth blew out either. But when I saw that only the skin was left on the ship's cat, and that he himself was flying off completely naked toward the Far East, I began to feel a little unpleasant."

"I have a book about a shipwreck," said Tommy. "It's called *Robinson Crusoe.*"

"Oh, yes, it's so good," said Annika. "Robinson— *he* came to a desert island."

"Have you ever been shipwrecked," asked Tommy, making himself a little more comfortable in the woodbox, "and landed on a desert island?"

"I should say I have!" said Pippi emphatically. "You'd have to hunt far and wide to find anyone as shipwrecked as I. Robinson's got nothing on me. I should think that there are only about eight or ten islands in the Atlantic and the Pacific that I have *not* landed on after shipwrecks. They are in a special blacklist in the tourists' books."

"Isn't it wonderful to be on a desert island?" asked Tommy. "I'd so much like to be shipwrecked just once!"

"That's easily arranged," said Pippi. "There's no shortage of islands."

"No—I know one not at all far away from here," said Tommy.

"Is it in a lake?" asked Pippi.

"Sure," said Tommy.

"Swell!" said Pippi. "For if it had been on dry land it would have been no good."

Tommy was wild with excitement. "Let's get shipwrecked!" he cried. "Let's go now, right away!"

In two days Tommy's and Annika's summer vacation was to begin, and at the same time their mother and father were going away. You couldn't find a better time to play Robinson Crusoe!

"If you're going to be shipwrecked you first have to have a boat," said Pippi.

"And we haven't any," said Annika.

"I saw an old, broken rowboat lying at the bottom of the river," said Pippi.

"But that has already been shipwrecked," said Annika.

"So much the better," said Pippi. "Then it knows what to do."

It was a simple matter for Pippi to pull out the sunken rowboat. She spent a whole day down by the river, mending the boat with boards and tar, and one rainy morning in the woodshed, making a pair of oars.

Tommy's and Annika's vacation began, and their parents went away.

"We'll be home in two days," said the children's mother. "Now be very good and obedient and remember that you must do just as Ella says."

Ella was the maid, and she was going to look after Tommy and Annika while their mother and father were away. But when the children were alone with Ella, Tommy said, "You don't need to look after us at all, because we're going to be with Pippi the whole time."

"We can look after ourselves," said Annika. "Pippi never has anyone to look after her. Why can't we be left alone for two days at least?"

Ella had no objection to having a couple of days off, and when Tommy and Annika had begged and teased long enough, Ella said she would go home and visit with her mother a while. But the children must promise to eat and sleep properly and not run out at night without putting on warm sweaters. Tommy said he would gladly put on a dozen sweaters, if only Ella would leave them alone.

So Ella left, and two hours later Pippi, Tommy and Annika, the horse, and Mr. Nilsson started on their trip to the desert island.

It was a mild evening in early summer. The air was warm, although the sky was cloudy. They had to walk quite a way before they came to the lake where the desert island was. Pippi carried the boat on her head. She had loaded an enormous sack and a tent on the horse's back.

"What's in the sack?" asked Tommy.

"Food and firearms, a blanket and an empty bottle," said Pippi, "for I think we ought to have quite a comfortable shipwreck, since it's your first one. Otherwise when I'm shipwrecked I usually shoot an antelope or a llama and eat the meat raw, but there might not be any antelopes or llamas on this island, and it would be a shame if we should have to starve to death just on account of a little thing like that."

"What are you going to use the empty bottle for?" asked Annika.

"What am I going to use the empty bottle for? How can you ask anything so stupid? A boat is, of course, the most important thing when you're going to be shipwrecked, but next comes an empty bottle. My father taught me that when I was still in the cradle. 'Pippi,' he said, 'it doesn't matter if you forget to wash your feet when you're going to be presented at Court, but if you forget the empty bottle when you're going to be shipwrecked, you might as well give up.' "

"Yes, but what are you going to use it for?" insisted Annika.

"Haven't you ever heard of a bottle letter? You write a letter and ask for help," said Pippi. "Then you stuff it in the bottle, put the stopper in, and throw the bottle into the water. And then it floats to someone who can come and save you. How on earth do you think you could be saved otherwise? Leave everything to chance? No, sir!"

"Oh, I see," said Annika.

Soon they came to the edge of the little lake, and

there in the middle of the lake was the desert island. The sun was just breaking through the clouds, throwing a warm glow over the early summer foliage.

"Really," said Pippi, "this is one of the nicest desert islands I've ever seen."

She quickly launched the boat onto the lake, lifted the pack off the horse, and stuffed everything into the bottom of the boat. Annika and Tommy and Mr. Nilsson jumped in.

Pippi patted the horse. "My dear horse, no matter how much I would like it, I cannot ask you to sit in the bottom of the boat. I hope you can swim. It's very simple. Look!"

Pippi jumped into the lake with all her clothes on and swam a few strokes. "It's lots of fun, you know, and if you want to have still more fun you can play whale, like this."

Pippi filled her mouth with water, lay on her back, and squirted like a fountain. The horse didn't look as if he thought it would be much fun, but when Pippi crawled into the boat, took the oars, and rowed off, the horse threw himself into the water and swam after her. He didn't play whale, though.

When they had almost reached the island, Pippi yelled, "Man all the pumps!"

And the next second: "In vain! We'll have to leave the ship. Every man for himself!"

She stepped up on the back seat of the boat and dived head first into the water. Soon she came up again, took hold of the rope on the boat, and swam for shore.

"I have to save the provisions anyway, so the crew might as well stay on board," she said.

She tied the rope around a stone and helped Tommy and Annika ashore. Mr. Nilsson rescued himself.

"A miracle has happened!" cried Pippi. "We are saved—at least for the time being, unless there are cannibals and lions on this island."

Even the horse had now reached the island. He got out of the water and shook himself.

"Good! here comes the first mate too," said Pippi. "Let us all hold a council of war."

Out of the sack she took a pistol which she had once found in a sea chest up in the attic. Holding the pistol straight in front of her, ready to fire, she sneaked about, looking carefully in all directions.

"What's the matter, Pippi?" asked Annika worriedly.

"I thought I heard the growling of a cannibal," said Pippi. "You can never be careful enough. What

would be the use of saving yourself from drowning only to be served with stewed vegetables for a cannibal's dinner?"

No cannibals were to be seen.

"Aha! they have retreated and taken cover," said Pippi. "Or perhaps they are sitting looking through their cookbooks to learn how they could cook us. And I'll tell you this, if they serve me with stewed carrots I'll never forgive them—I *hate* carrots."

"Oh, Pippi, don't talk like that!" said Annika, shivering.

"Oh, don't you like carrots either? Well, anyway, let's put up the tent now."

Pippi put up the tent in a sheltered place, and Tommy and Annika crept in and out of it and were perfectly happy. A short distance from the tent, Pippi placed some stones in a ring, and on top of these sticks and pine cones.

"Oh! how wonderful! Are we going to have a fire?" asked Annika.

"Yes, sirree!" said Pippi. She took two pieces of wood and started to rub them together.

Tommy was much interested. "Oh, Pippi!" he said, delighted. "Are you going to make a fire the way they do in the jungles?"

"No, but my fingers are cold," said Pippi, "and

this is a good way to warm them. Let me see, where did I put the matches?"

Soon a bright fire was burning, and Tommy said he thought it was awfully cozy.

"Yes, and besides, it will keep the wild animals away," said Pippi.

Annika drew in her breath sharply. "What wild animals?" she asked with a tremor in her voice.

"The mosquitoes," said Pippi and thoughtfully scratched a large mosquito bite on her leg.

Annika sighed with relief.

"Yes, and the lions too, of course," continued Pippi. "I don't think it will help against pythons or against the American buffalo."

She patted her pistol. "But don't worry, Annika," she said. "With this I'll surely be able to defend us even if we should be attacked by a field mouse."

Then Pippi got out coffee and sandwiches, and the children sat around the fire and ate and enjoyed themselves immensely. Mr. Nilsson sat on Pippi's shoulder and ate too, and the horse stuck out his nose from time to time and got a piece of bread and a lump of sugar. There was also lots of tender green grass for him to eat.

The sky was cloudy and it began to grow dark. Annika moved up as near to Pippi as she could get. The flames threw strange shadows. It seemed as if

the darkness were alive outside the little circle that
was lighted by the fire. Annika shivered. Just suppose a cannibal was standing behind that bush, or a
lion hiding behind the big stone over there!

Pippi put down her coffee cup. "Fifteen men on
a dead man's chest, yo, ho, ho! and a bottle of
rum," she sang in her deep, hoarse voice. Annika
shivered more than ever.

"I have that song in another one of my books—a
pirate book," said Tommy eagerly.

"Really?" said Pippi. "Then it must be Fridolf who
wrote that book, for he taught me the song. How
often I've sat on the after deck of my father's ship
on starlit nights, with the Southern Cross right over
my head, and Fridolf beside me, singing. Fifteen
men on a dead man's chest, yo, ho, ho! and a bottle
of rum" sang Pippi once more with an even
hoarser voice.

"Pippi, I feel so funny inside me when you sing
like that," said Tommy. "It feels so terrible and so
wonderful at the same time."

"It feels almost only terrible inside me," said
Annika, "but a little wonderful too."

"I'm going to sea when I get big," said Tommy
decidedly. "I'm going to be a pirate just like you,
Pippi."

"Swell!" said Pippi. "The Terror of the Caribbean! That'll be you and me, Tommy. We'll plunder gold and jewels and precious stones and we'll have a hiding place for our treasures way in a cave on a desert island in the Pacific Ocean, and three skeletons to watch the cave. We'll have a flag with a skull and crossbones, and we'll sing 'Fifteen men on a dead man's chest' so that you can hear it from one end of the Atlantic to the other, and all seafaring men will turn pale when they hear us and think about throwing themselves into the sea to avoid our bloody, bloody revenge."

"But what about me?" asked Annika complainingly. "I don't dare become a pirate. What'll I do then?"

"Oh, you can come along anyway," said Pippi, "and dust the grand piano."

After a while the fire died down. "Time to go to bed," said Pippi. She had put spruce boughs on the ground under the tent, and on top of the spruce boughs several thick blankets.

"Do you want to sleep with us in the tent," Pippi asked the horse, "or would you rather stand out here under a tree with a blanket over you? Oh, so you always feel sick when you sleep in a tent? Okay, just as you like!" Pippi gave him a friendly pat.

Soon all three children and Mr. Nilsson lay rolled

up in blankets in the tent. Outside the waves lapped against the shore.

"Hear the ocean breakers!" said Pippi dreamily.

It was as dark as pitch, and Annika held Pippi's hand, for everything seemed less dangerous then. Suddenly it began to rain. The raindrops splashed on the tent, but inside everything was warm and dry, and it seemed very pleasant to hear the pitter-patter of the raindrops. Pippi went out and put another blanket on the horse. He stood under a thick spruce tree, so he kept pretty dry.

"Isn't this wonderful?" Tommy sighed when Pippi came in again.

"Sure!" said Pippi. "And look what I found under a stone—three chocolate bars!"

Three minutes later Annika was asleep with her mouth full of chocolate and her hand in Pippi's.

"We forgot to brush our teeth tonight," said Tommy, and then he too fell asleep.

When Tommy and Annika woke up, Pippi had disappeared. They hurried to crawl out of the tent. The sun was shining brightly. In front of the tent a new fire was burning and Pippi was squatting by the fire, frying ham and boiling coffee.

"Congratulations and Happy Easter!" she called when she saw Tommy and Annika.

"Oh, it's not Easter now," said Tommy.

"Isn't it? Save the wish until next year, then," Pippi replied.

The good smell of ham and coffee tickled the children's nostrils. They squatted around the fire, and Pippi passed around ham and eggs and potatoes, after which they drank coffee and ate molasses cookies and never had a breakfast tasted so wonderful.

"I think we have it better than Robinson Crusoe," said Tommy.

"Yes, and if we could only get a little fresh fish for dinner I'm afraid Robinson Crusoe would be green with envy," said Pippi.

"Ugh! I don't like fish," said Tommy.

"I don't either," said Annika.

But Pippi cut off a long, narrow branch, tied a string to one end, made a hook out of a pin, and put a piece of bread on the hook and herself on a large stone down near the water's edge.

"Now we'll see," she said.

"What will you fish for?" asked Tommy.

"Octopus," said Pippi. "That's a delicacy beyond compare."

She sat there a whole hour, but no octopus bit. A perch came up and sniffed at the piece of bread, but Pippi quickly drew up the hook.

"No, thank you, my boy," she said. "When I say octopus I mean octopus, and you shouldn't come stealing the bait."

After a while Pippi threw the fishpole into the lake. "You were lucky," she said. "We'll have to eat pancakes. The octopuses are stubborn today." Tommy and Annika were satisfied.

The water glistened invitingly in the sun. "Shall we go for a swim?" asked Tommy.

Pippi and Annika were game. The water was quite cold. Tommy and Annika stuck their big toes in, but quickly pulled them out again.

"I know a better way," said Pippi. There was a rock quite near the shore, and on top of the rock was a tree. The branches of the tree stretched themselves out over the water. Pippi climbed up into the tree and tied a rope around a branch. "Like this—see?"

She took hold of the rope, swung herself out, and dropped into the water.

"You get ducked all over at once, this way," she cried as her head came up out of the water.

Tommy and Annika were a little doubtful at first, but it looked like so much fun that they decided to try it, and when they had tried it once they never wanted to stop, for it was even more fun than it looked. Mr. Nilsson wanted to try too. He slid down the rope, but just before he reached the water he turned and scampered back up at a terrific pace. He did this each time, although the children called to him and told him that he was a coward. Then Pippi found that you could sit on a piece of board and slide down into the water, and that was fun too, for it made a terrific splash when you landed.

"That Robinson Crusoe, did he slide down a piece of board too? I wonder," said Pippi as she sat at the top of the rock ready to take off.

"No—it doesn't say so in the book, at least," said Tommy.

"Well, that's what I thought. I don't think there was much to his shipwreck. What did he do all day, cross-stitch embroidery? Here I come!"

Pippi slid down into the water, with her red braids streaming out behind her.

After their swim the children decided to explore the desert island thoroughly. All three got on the horse, and he jogged off good-naturedly. Up hill and down dale they rode, through the underbrush and between clumps of spruce, through marshes and over pretty little clearings where the grass was thick with wild flowers. Pippi sat with the pistol ready, and from time to time she fired a shot so that the horse jumped high into the air with fright.

"There! I shot a lion!" she said with satisfaction.

Or: "Now that cannibal has planted his last potato."

"I think this island should be ours forever," said Tommy when they returned to the camp and Pippi had started to make pancakes. Pippi and Annika thought so too.

The pancakes tasted wonderful when you ate them steaming hot. There were no plates and no knives or forks, and Annika asked, "May we eat with our fingers?"

"It's all right with me if you do," said Pippi, "but for my part I'll stick to the old method of eating with my mouth."

"Oh, you know what I mean, silly!" said Annika. She took a pancake in her hand and put it in her mouth with great enjoyment.

And then night came again. The fire burned down. Snuggled close to each other, their faces smeared with pancake, the children lay in their blankets. A big star shone through a crack in the tent. The "ocean breakers" lulled them to sleep.

"We have to go home today," said Tommy sadly the next morning.

"Isn't it a shame!" said Annika. "I would like to stay here all summer, but Mommy and Daddy are coming home today."

After breakfast Tommy went exploring down by

the shore. Suddenly he gave a loud cry. The boat! It was gone!

Annika was much upset. How would they ever be able to get away from there? She did want to be on the island all summer, but it was different when you knew that you couldn't go home. And what would poor Mommy say when she found that Tommy and Annika had disappeared? Annika's eyes filled with tears when she thought about it.

"What's the matter with you, Annika?" asked Pippi. "What is your idea of a shipwreck anyway? What do you think Robinson Crusoe would have said if a ship had come along and picked him up when he had been on the desert island only two days? 'Here you are, Mr. Crusoe, please come aboard and be saved and bathed and shaved and get your toenails cut.' No, thank you. I think surely Mr. Crusoe would have run and hidden behind a bush. For if you've at last landed on a desert island you would like to stay there at least seven years."

"Seven years!" Annika shivered, and Tommy looked thoughtful.

"Well I don't mean that we should stay here forever," said Pippi comfortingly. "When Tommy has to go to military school we'll have to let folks know where we are, I guess, but perhaps he can get a year or two's postponement."

Annika became more and more desperate. Pippi looked at her searchingly. "Well, if you're going to take it like that, there's nothing for us to do but send off the bottle letter."

She dug the empty bottle out of the sack. She also managed to find some paper and a pencil. Putting these on a stone in front of Tommy, she said, "You know more about the art of writing than I do."

"But what shall I write?" asked Tommy.

"Let me think a moment." Pippi pondered. "You can write this: 'Help us before we perish—we have been on this island for two days without snuff.'"

"Oh, but Pippi, we can't write that!" said Tommy reproachfully. "It isn't true."

"What isn't true?"

"We can't write 'without snuff,'" said Tommy.

"Oh, we can't?" said Pippi. "Have you any snuff?"

"No," said Tommy.

"Has Annika any snuff?"

"No, of course not—but—"

"Have I any snuff?" continued Pippi.

"No, maybe you haven't," said Tommy, "but we don't use snuff."

"Well, that's just what I want you to write: 'We've been without snuff for two days.'"

"Yes, but if we write that people will think we use snuff," insisted Tommy.

"Now look here, Tommy," said Pippi, "will you just answer this. Which people are more often without snuff—the ones who use it or the ones who don't?"

"The ones who don't, of course," said Tommy.

"Well, what are you fussing about, then?" asked Pippi. "Write it as I tell you."

So Tommy wrote: "Help us before we perish— we have been on this island for two days without snuff."

Pippi took the paper, stuffed it into the bottle, put the stopper in, and threw the bottle into the water.

"Now we should soon be rescued," she said.

The bottle floated off but shortly came to rest, caught in some tree roots near the shore.

"We'll have to throw it out farther," said Tommy.

"That would be the most stupid thing we could do," said Pippi, "for if it floats far away our rescuers won't know where to look for us. But if it lies here we can call to them when they have found it, and then we'll be rescued right away."

Pippi sat down by the shore. "It's best that we keep our eyes on the bottle the whole time," she said.

Tommy and Annika sat down beside her. After ten minutes Pippi said impatiently, "People must think that we haven't anything else to do but sit here and wait to get rescued. Where can they be, anyway?"

"What people?" asked Annika.

"The ones who are going to rescue us," said Pippi. "It's unforgivable when you consider that human lives are at stake."

Annika began to believe that they really were going to perish on the island, but suddenly Pippi raised her finger in the air and cried, "My goodness, but I'm thoughtless! How could I forget it?"

"What?" asked Tommy.

"The boat!" said Pippi: "I carried it up on shore last night after you had gone to sleep."

"But why did you do that?" asked Annika reproachfully.

"I was afraid that it might get wet," said Pippi.

In a jiffy she had fetched the boat, which lay well hidden under a spruce. She shoved it into the lake and said grimly, "There! Now the rescuers can come! For when they come to rescue us they'll come in vain, because now we are rescuing ourselves, and that will just be a good one on them. It will teach them to hurry up the next time."

"I hope we'll get home before Mommy and Daddy," said Annika when they were in the boat and Pippi was rowing toward shore with strong strokes. "How worried Mommy will be otherwise!"

"I don't think she will," said Pippi.

Mr. and Mrs. Settergren got home half an hour before the children. No Tommy and Annika were in sight, but in the mailbox was a piece of paper on which was printed

FOR GUDNES SAK DONT TINK YUR CHIL-
DRUN R DED R LOS THEY R NT ATAL THEY
R JUS ALITTAL SHIPREKED AN WIL SUN CUM
HOM I SWER.

GRITINS FRUM

PIPPI

7

Pippi Gets Unexpected Company

One summer evening Pippi, Tommy, and Annika sat on the steps of Pippi's porch, eating wild strawberries which they had picked that morning. It was a lovely evening, with birds singing and the perfume of the flowers—and the strawberries. Everything was peaceful. The children ate and said hardly a word. Tommy and Annika were thinking how lovely it was that it was summer and how nice that school wouldn't start for a long time. What Pippi thought about, no one knows.

"Pippi, now you have lived here in Villa Villekulla a whole year," said Annika suddenly, hugging Pippi's arm.

"Yes, time flies and one begins to grow old," said Pippi. "This autumn I'll be ten, and then I guess I'll have seen my best days."

"Do you think you will live here always?" asked Tommy. "I mean until you're old enough to become a pirate?"

"No one knows," said Pippi. "I don't suppose my father will stay on that island forever. As soon as he gets a boat made he'll surely come for me."

Tommy and Annika sighed.

Suddenly Pippi sat upright on the steps. "Look, there he comes now!" she exclaimed, pointing toward the gate. She covered the garden walk in three leaps. Tommy and Annika followed her hesitatingly, just in time to see her throw herself on the neck of a very fat gentleman with a short red mustache and blue sailor pants.

"Papa Efraim!" cried Pippi, waving her legs so eagerly as she hung around his neck that her big shoes fell off. "Papa Efraim, how you have grown!"

"Pippilotta Delicatessa Windowshade Mackrelmint Efraim's Daughter Longstocking, my beloved child! I was just going to say that you have grown."

"I knew that," said Pippi. "That's why I said it first. Ha, ha!"

"My child, are you just as strong as you used to be?"

"Stronger," said Pippi. "Shall we Indian wrestle?"

"Go ahead!" said Papa Efraim.

There was a table in the garden, and there Pippi and her father sat down to lock arms while Tommy and Annika looked on. There was only one person in the world who was as strong as Pippi, and that was her father. There they sat, bending with all their might, but neither succeeded in bending the other's arm.

At last Captain Longstocking's arm began to tremble a little, and Pippi said, "When I'm ten I'll bend your arm, Papa Efraim."

Papa Efraim thought so too.

"Oh, my goodness!" said Pippi. "I forgot all about introducing you. This is Tommy and Annika, and this is my father, the Captain and His Majesty, Efraim Longstocking, because you are a cannibal king, aren't you, Papa?"

"That's right," said Captain Longstocking. "I am king over the Kurrekurredutt natives on an island known as the Kurrekurredutt Island. I floated ashore there after I had been blown into the water, you remember."

"Well, that's just what I knew all along. I never believed that you were drowned."

"Drowned! I should say not! It's just as impossible for me to drown as for a camel to thread a needle. I float on my fat."

Tommy and Annika looked at Captain Longstocking wonderingly. "Why aren't you wearing cannibal king clothes?" asked Tommy.

"Oh, I have them here in my bag," said Captain Longstocking.

"Oh, put them on, please put them on!" cried Pippi. "I want to see my father in royal robes."

They all went into the kitchen. Captain Longstocking disappeared into Pippi's bedroom, and the children sat on the woodbox, waiting.

"It's just like at the theater," said Annika, excitedly.

Then—*pang!*—the door opened and there stood the cannibal king! He had a grass skirt around his middle, and on his head he wore a crown of gold! Around his neck hung many strands of big colored beads. In one hand he held a spear, and in the other a shield. Under the grass skirt a couple of fat, hairy legs stuck out, with thick gold bracelets on the ankles.

"*Ussamkussor mussor filibussor,*" said Captain Longstocking, frowning threateningly.

"Oh, he speaks native language!" said Tommy, delighted. "What does that mean, Uncle Efraim?"

"It means 'Tremble, my enemies!'"

"Listen, Papa Efraim," said Pippi. "Weren't the people surprised when you floated ashore on their island?"

"Yes, terribly surprised," answered Captain Longstocking. "First they wanted to eat me, but when I had torn down a palm tree with my bare hands they changed their minds and made me king. After that I ruled in the mornings and built my boat in the afternoons. It took a long time to finish it, as

I had to do everything all by myself. It was just a little sailboat, of course. When it was finished I told the people I had to leave them for a little while but that I would soon come back and then I would have a princess with me, whose name was Pippilotta. Then they beat on their shields and shouted, '*Ussomplussor, ussomplussor!*' "

"What does that mean?" asked Annika.

"It means 'Bravo, bravo!' Then I ruled hard for two weeks so that it would last during the whole time I was away. And then I set sail, and the people cried '*Ussamkura kussomkara.*' That means 'Come back soon, fat white chief.' Then I steered straight for South Arabia, and what do you think was the first thing I saw when I jumped ashore there? My old faithful schooner, the *Hoptoad* and my faithful old Fridolf, standing by the rail and waving with all his might. 'Fridolf,' I said, 'now I will take command.' 'Aye, aye, Captain,' he said, and so I did. The whole old crew was there, and now the *Hoptoad* is down here in the harbor so you can go and see all your old friends, Pippi."

Pippi was so happy that she stood on her head on the kitchen table, kicking her legs. But Tommy and Annika couldn't help feeling a little sad. It was just as if someone were trying to take Pippi away from them, they thought.

"Now we'll celebrate," cried Pippi as she came down on her feet again. "Now we'll celebrate so that the whole house shakes!" And then she dished up a big supper, and everyone sat down at the kitchen table to eat. Pippi gobbled up three hard-boiled eggs with the shells on. From time to time she bit her Papa's ear, just because she was so happy to see him. Mr. Nilsson, who had been sleeping, came running out and rubbed his eyes in surprise when he saw Captain Longstocking.

"Well, I see you still have Mr. Nilsson," said Captain Longstocking.

"You bet, and I have another pet too," said Pippi. She went out and fetched the horse, who also got a hard-boiled egg to chew on.

Captain Longstocking was very glad that his daughter had settled herself so comfortably in Villa Villekulla, and he was glad that she had had her suitcase full of gold pieces, so that she had not been in need while he was away.

When everyone had eaten, Captain Longstocking took a tom-tom out of his bag. It was one that the natives used to beat time on for their dances and sacrificial feasts. Captain Longstocking sat down on the floor and beat on the drum. It sounded strange and weird, different from anything that Tommy and Annika had ever heard.

"Native-ish!" explained Tommy to Annika.

Pippi took off her big shoes and danced in her stocking feet, a dance that also was weird. Then King Efraim danced a wild war dance that he had learned on Kurrekurredutt Island. He swung his spear and waved his shield wildly, and his naked feet stomped so hard that Pippi cried, "Look out you don't break through the kitchen floor!"

"That doesn't matter," cried Captain Longstocking, and whirled along. "For now you are going to be a cannibal princess, my darling daughter."

Pippi jumped up and danced with her Papa. They danced back and forth facing each other, yelling and shouting, and from time to time leaping high into the air, so that Tommy and Annika were dizzy just from watching them. Mr. Nilsson must have become dizzy too, for he sat and held his hands over his eyes the whole time.

By and by the dance turned into a wrestling match between Pippi and her father. Captain Longstocking threw his daughter so that she landed on the hat shelf, but she didn't stay there long. With a wild cry she leaped across the kitchen and landed right on Papa Efraim, and the next second had tossed him so that he flew like a meteor, head first into the woodbox. His fat legs stuck right up in the air. He couldn't get out by himself, for in the first place he was too fat, and in the second place he was laughing so hard. A rumbling like thunder came from the woodbox.

Pippi took hold of his feet to pull him up, but then he laughed so he almost choked. He was so terribly ticklish!

"Don't ti—ck—l—e me!" he cried, giggling hysterically. "Throw me into the sea or throw me through the window, do anything, but don't ti—ck—l—e the bottoms of my feet!"

He laughed so that Tommy and Annika were afraid that the woodbox would burst. At last he managed to get out, and as soon as he was back on his feet he lunged at Pippi and threw her across the kitchen. She landed on her face on the stove, which was black with soot.

But she was up in an instant and threw herself at her father. She punched him so that the grass in his skirt came loose and flew all over the kitchen. The gold crown fell off and rolled under the table.

At last Pippi succeeded in getting her father down on the floor, and she sat on him and said, "Do you admit that I won?"

"Yes, you won," said Captain Longstocking, and then they both laughed till they cried. Pippi bit her Papa lightly on the nose, and he said, "I haven't

had so much fun since you and I got mixed up in that sailors' fight in Singapore."

He crawled under the table and picked up his crown. "The cannibals should see this," he said, "the royal crown lying under the kitchen table in Villa Villekulla."

He put on the crown and combed out his grass skirt, which looked rather scanty.

"You'll have to send that to invisible mending," said Pippi.

"Yes, but it was worth it," answered Captain Longstocking.

He sat down on the floor and wiped the perspiration from his forehead. "Well, Pippi, my child," he said, "do you ever lie nowadays?"

"Yes, when I have time, but it isn't very often," said Pippi modestly. "How about you? You weren't so backward about lying either."

"Well, I usually lie a little for the people on Saturday nights, if they have behaved well during the week. We usually have a little lie-and-song evening, with accompaniment of drums and firelight dances. The more I lie, the harder they beat the drums."

"Is that so?" asked Pippi. "No one here drums for me. Here I go in my loneliness and puff myself so full of lies that it is a pleasure to hear me, but no one even plays on a comb for me. The other night, when I had gone to bed, I lied a long story about a calf who crocheted lace and climbed trees, and just think, I believed every word of it! That I call good lying! But nobody beat a drum for me. Oh, no!"

"Well, then, I'll do it," said Captain Longstocking, and he beat a long riffle on the drum for his daughter, and Pippi sat on his knee and rubbed her sooty face against his cheek so that he became just as black as she was.

Annika was thinking about something. She didn't know if it was quite proper to say it, but she just had to. "It's not nice to lie," she said. "Mommy says that."

"Oh, how silly you are, Annika!" said Tommy. "Pippi doesn't really lie. She just lies for fun. She makes up things, don't you understand, stupid?"

Pippi looked thoughtfully at Tommy. "Sometimes you speak so wisely that I'm afraid you will become great," she said.

It was evening. Tommy and Annika had to go home. It had been a full day and it had been such fun to see a real live cannibal king, and of course it was nice for Pippi that her father had come home, but still . . . still . . .

When Tommy and Annika had crept off to bed,

they didn't lie there talking, as they usually did. There was absolute silence in the nursery.

Suddenly a sigh was heard. It was Tommy.

After a while another sigh was heard. This time it was Annika.

"What are you sighing about?" asked Tommy crossly.

But he didn't get an answer, for Annika was crying with her head under the quilt.

8
Pippi Has
a Farewell
Party

When Tommy and Annika came into the kitchen at Villa Villekulla the next morning, the whole house was resounding with the most terrible snores. Captain Longstocking was not yet awake, but Pippi stood in the middle of the kitchen floor, doing her morning exercises. She was just turning her fifteenth somersault when Tommy and Annika interrupted her.

"Well, now I don't have to worry about my future any more," said Pippi. "I'm going to be a cannibal princess. Yes, for half the year I'm going to be a cannibal princess and half the year I'm going to sail around on all the oceans of the world on the *Hoptoad.* Papa thinks that if he rules hard half the year, the people will get along without a king during the other half; for you know an old sea dog like him has to feel a deck under his feet occasionally, and then he has to think about my education too. If

I'm going to be a really good pirate, it wouldn't do to spend all my time at court. That's weakening, Papa says."

"Aren't you going to spend any time at all in Villa Villekulla?" asked Tommy sadly.

"Yes, when we've retired and got a pension," answered Pippi, "in about fifty or sixty years. Then we'll play and have lots of fun, won't we?"

This wasn't much comfort to Tommy and Annika.

"Just think, a cannibal princess!" said Pippi dreamily. "Not many children get to be that. Oh, I'll be so fine, I'll have rings in my ears and a little larger ring in my nose."

"What else are you going to wear?" asked Annika.

"Not another thing," answered Pippi. "Never anything else."

She sighed ecstatically. "Princess Pippilotta! What a life! What glamour! And how I shall dance! Princess Pippilotta dances in the firelight to the beating of the drums! Just imagine how my nose ring will jingle!"

"When—when are you going to leave?" asked Tommy. His voice sounded a bit rusty.

"The *Hoptoad* is lifting anchor tomorrow," said Pippi.

All three children were silent a long while; there

didn't seem to be anything more to say. At last, however, Pippi turned another somersault and said, "But tonight we'll have a farewell party in Villa Villekulla—a farewell party! I say no more. All who want to come to say good-by to me are welcome."

The news spread like wildfire among all the children in the little town.

"Pippi Longstocking is going to leave town, and she is having a farewell party tonight in Villa Villekulla. Everyone who wants to may go to the party."

There were several who wanted to—in fact there were thirty-four children. Tommy and Annika had persuaded their mother to promise that they could stay up as long as they wanted to that night. She understood that this was absolutely necessary.

Tommy and Annika would never forget the evening of Pippi's farewell party. It was one of those wonderful warm and beautiful summer evenings when you say to yourself, "Ah, this is summer!" All the roses in Pippi's garden glowed in the fragrant dusk. The wind whispered softly in the old trees. Everything would have been wonderful if only—if only—Tommy and Annika couldn't bear to finish the thought.

All the children from town had brought their bird whistles and were playing merrily as they came up the garden walk of Villa Villekulla. Tommy and Annika led them. Just as they reached the porch steps, the door was flung open and Pippi stood on the threshold. Her eyes gleamed in her freckled face.

"Welcome to my humble dwelling!" she said and threw out her arms.

Annika looked at her closely so that she would always remember just how Pippi looked. Never, never would she forget her as she stood there with her red braids and freckles and her happy smile and her big black shoes.

In the distance was heard a soft beating on a drum. Captain Longstocking sat in the kitchen with his native drum between his knees. He was wearing his royal robes today too. Pippi had especially asked him to. She realized that all the children wanted to see a real live cannibal king.

The whole kitchen was soon full of children staring at King Efraim, and Annika thought that it was a good thing no more had come, for there wouldn't have been room for them. Just as she was thinking this, the music of an accordion was heard from the garden, and in came the whole crew from the *Hoptoad*, led by Fridolf. It was he who was playing the accordion. Pippi had been down to the harbor that day to see her friends and had asked them to come to the farewell party.

Now she rushed at Fridolf and hugged him until

he was blue in the face. Then she let go of him and cried, "Music! Music!"

Fridolf played on his accordion, King Efraim beat his drum, and all the children blew their bird whistles.

The lid on the woodbox was closed, and on it stood long rows of bottles of soda. On the large kitchen table were fifteen layer cakes covered with whipped cream, and on the stove a huge kettle full of hot dogs.

King Efraim began by grabbing eight hot dogs. All the others followed his example, and soon nothing was heard in the kitchen except the sound of people eating hot dogs. Afterward each child was allowed to help himself to all the soda and layer cake he wanted.

It was a little crowded in the kitchen, so the guests spread out onto the porch and even into the garden. The whipped cream on the cake shone white in the dusk.

When everyone had eaten as much as he could, Tommy suggested that they should shake down the hot dogs and cake by playing a game—Follow the Leader, for instance. Pippi didn't know that game, but Tommy explained to her that one person would be the leader and all the rest had to do everything that the leader did.

"Okay," said Pippi. "That sounds like fun, and

it would probably be best for me to be the leader."

She began by climbing up on the laundry roof. To get there she first had to climb up on the garden fence and then crawl up the roof on her stomach. Pippi and Tommy and Annika had done this so often that it was easy for them, but the other children thought it was rather difficult. The sailors from the *Hoptoad* were used to climbing up the masts, so they made the roof without any trouble, but it was quite an ordeal for Captain Longstocking because he was so fat, and besides his grass skirt kept getting caught. He panted and puffed as he heaved himself up on the roof.

"This grass skirt will never be the same again," he said sadly.

From the laundry roof Pippi jumped down to the ground. Some of the smaller children didn't dare do this, but Fridolf was so nice that he lifted down all those who were afraid to jump. Then Pippi turned six somersaults on the lawn. Everyone did the same, but Captain Longstocking said, "Someone will have to give me a push from behind, or I'll never be able to do it."

Pippi did. She gave him such a big push that once he got started he couldn't stop, but rolled like a ball across the lawn and turned fourteen somersaults instead of six.

Then Pippi rushed up the porch steps and into Villa Villekulla, climbed out through a window, and, by spreading her legs far apart managed to reach a ladder that stood outside. She ran quickly up the ladder, jumped onto the roof of Villa Villekulla, ran along the ridgepole, jumped up onto the chimney, stood on one leg and crowed like a rooster, threw herself down head first into a tree that stood near the corner of the house, slid down to the ground, rushed into the woodshed, took an ax and chopped a board out of the wall, crept through the narrow opening, jumped up on the garden fence, walked along the fence for fifty yards, climbed up into an oak, and sat down to rest at the very top of the tree.

Quite a crowd had gathered in the street outside Villa Villekulla, and when the people went home they told everyone that they had seen a cannibal king standing on one leg on the chimney of Villa Villekulla, crowing "Cock-a-doodle-do!" so that you could hear it far and wide. Of course no one believed them.

When Captain Longstocking tried to squeeze himself through the narrow opening in the woodshed, the inevitable happened—he stuck and couldn't get either out or in. This, of course, broke up the game, and all the children stood around, watching Fridolf cut Captain Longstocking out of the wall.

"That was a mighty good game," said Captain Longstocking, laughing, when he was free at last. "What are we going to play next?"

"In the good old days on the ship," said Fridolf, "Captain Longstocking and Pippi used to have a contest to see which was the strongest. It was a lot of fun to watch them."

"That's a good idea," said Captain Longstocking, "but the trouble is that my daughter is getting to be stronger than I."

Tommy was standing next to Pippi. "Pippi," he whispered, "I was so afraid you would climb down into our hiding place in the hollow oak when you played Follow the Leader, for I don't want anyone to find out about it, even if we never go there again."

"No, that's our own secret," said Pippi.

Her father took hold of an iron rod and bent it in the middle as if it were made of wax. Pippi took another iron rod and did the same.

"Fiddlesticks!" said Pippi. "I used to amuse myself with these simple tricks when I was still in the cradle, just to pass the time away."

Captain Longstocking then lifted off the kitchen door. Fridolf and seven of the other sailors stood on the door, and Captain Longstocking lifted them high into the air and carried them around the lawn ten times.

It was now quite dark, and Pippi lighted torches here and there. They looked very pretty and cast a magic glow over the garden.

"Are you ready?" she said to her father after the tenth trip around the garden. He was.

Then Pippi put the horse on the kitchen door and told Fridolf and three other sailors to get on the horse. Each of the sailors held two children in his arms. Fridolf held Tommy and Annika. Then Pippi lifted the door and carried it around the lawn twenty-five times. It looked splendid in the light of the torches.

"Well, child, you certainly *are* stronger than I," said Captain Longstocking.

Afterward everyone sat down on the lawn. Fridolf played his accordion and all the other sailors sang the prettiest chanties. The children danced to the music. Pippi took two torches in her hands and danced more wildly than anyone else.

The party ended with fireworks. Pippi fired off rockets and pinwheels that lighted up the whole sky. Annika sat on the porch and looked on. It was so beautiful, so lovely! She couldn't see the roses, but she smelled their fragrance in the dark. How wonderful everything would have been if—if—Annika felt as if a cold hand were gripping her heart. Tomorrow—how would it be then, and the whole summer vacation, and forever? There would be no more Pippi in Villa Villekulla, there would be no Mr. Nilsson, and no horse would stand on the porch. No more horseback rides, no more picnics with Pippi, no more cozy evenings in the kitchen at Villa Villekulla, no tree with soda growing in it—well, the tree would of course still be there, but Annika had a strong feeling that no more soda would grow there when Pippi was gone. What would Tommy and she do tomorrow? Play croquet, probably. Annika sighed.

The party was over. All the children thanked Pippi and said goodnight. Captain Longstocking went back to the *Hoptoad* with his sailors. He thought that Pippi might just as well come along with them, but Pippi wanted to sleep one more night in Villa Villekulla.

"Tomorrow at ten we weigh anchor. Don't forget," cried Captain Longstocking as he left.

Pippi, Tommy, and Annika were alone. They sat on the porch steps in the dark, perfectly quiet.

"You can come here and play, anyway," said Pippi at last. "The key will be hanging on a nail beside the door. You can take everything in the chest drawers, and if I put a ladder inside the oak you can climb down there yourselves, but perhaps there won't be so much soda growing there—it's not the season for it now."

"No, Pippi," said Tommy seriously, "we won't come here any more."

"No, never, never," said Annika, and she thought that in the future she would close her eyes every time she passed Villa Villekulla. Villa Villekulla without Pippi—Annika felt that cold hand around her heart again.

9
Pippi
Goes Aboard

Pippi locked the door of Villa Villekulla carefully and hung the key on a nail beside the door; then she lifted the horse down from the porch—for the last time, she lifted him down from the porch. Mr. Nilsson already sat on her shoulder, looking important. He probably understood that something special was going to happen.

"Well, I guess that's all," said Pippi.

Tommy and Annika nodded. "Yes, I guess it is."

"It's still early," said Pippi. "Let's walk; that will take longer."

Tommy and Annika nodded again, but they didn't say anything. Then they started walking toward the town, toward the harbor, toward the *Hoptoad.* The horse jogged slowly along behind them.

Pippi glanced over her shoulder at Villa Villekulla. "Nice little place," she said. "No fleas, clean and comfortable, and that's probably more than you can say about the clay hut where I'll be living in the future."

Tommy and Annika said nothing.

"If there are an awful lot of fleas in my hut," continued Pippi, "I'll train them and keep them in a cigar box and play Run, Sheep, Run with them at night. I'll tie little bows around their legs, and the two most faithful and affectionate fleas I will call Tommy and Annika, and they shall sleep with me at night."

Not even this could make Tommy and Annika more talkative.

"What on earth is wrong with you?" asked Pippi irritably. "I tell you it's dangerous to keep quiet too long. Tongues dry up if you don't use them. In Calcutta I once knew a potter who never said a word. And once when he wanted to say to me, 'Good-by, dear Pippi, happy journey and thanks for your visit,' he opened his mouth and can you guess what he said? First he made some horrible faces, for the hinges to his mouth had rusted and I had to grease them for him with a little sewing-machine oil, and then a sound came out: 'U buy uye muy.' I looked in his mouth, and, imagine! there lay his tongue like a little wilted leaf, and as long as he lived that potter could never say anything but 'U buy uye muy.' It would be awful if the same thing should happen to you. Let me see if you can say this better than the potter did: 'Happy journey, dear Pippi, and thanks for your visit.' Go on, try it."

"Happy journey, dear Pippi, and thanks for your visit," said Tommy and Annika obediently.

"Thank goodness for that," said Pippi. "You certainly gave me a scare. If you had said 'U buy uye muy' I don't know what I would have done."

There was the harbor, there lay the *Hoptoad*. Captain Longstocking stood on deck, shouting out his commands, the sailors ran back and forth to make everything ready for their departure. All the people in the little town had crowded on the dock to wave good-by to Pippi, and here she came with Tommy and Annika and the horse and Mr. Nilsson.

"Here comes Pippi Longstocking! Make way for Pippi Longstocking!" cried the crowd and made a path for Pippi to come through.

Pippi nodded and smiled to the left and the right. Then she took up the horse and carried him up the gangplank. The poor animal looked around suspiciously, for horses don't care very much for boat rides.

"Well, here you are, my beloved child!" called Captain Longstocking and broke off in the middle of a command to embrace Pippi. He folded her in his arms, and they hugged each other until their ribs cracked.

Annika had gone around with a lump in her throat all morning, and when she saw Pippi lift the horse aboard, the lump loosened. She began to cry as she stood there squeezed against a packing case on the dock, first quietly and then more and more desperately.

"Don't bawl!" said Tommy angrily. "You'll shame us in front of all the people here."

The result of this was only to make Annika burst out in a regular torrent of tears. She cried so that she shook. Tommy kicked a stone so that it rolled across the dock and fell into the water. He really would have liked to throw it at the *Hoptoad*—that mean old boat that was going to take Pippi away from them. Really, if no one had been looking, Tommy would have liked to cry also, but a boy just couldn't let people see him cry. He kicked away another stone.

Pippi came running down the gangplank and rushed over to Tommy and Annika. She took their hands in hers. "Ten minutes left," she said.

Then Annika threw herself across the packing case and cried as if her heart would break. There were no more stones for Tommy to kick, so he clenched his teeth and looked murderous.

All the children in the little town gathered around Pippi. They took out their bird whistles and blew a farewell tune for her. It sounded sad beyond words, for it was a very, very mournful tune. Annika was crying so hard that she could hardly catch her breath.

Just then Tommy remembered that he had written a farewell poem for Pippi and he pulled out a paper and began to read. It was terrible that his voice should shake so.

> *Good-by, dear Pippi, you from us go.*
> *You may look high and you may look low,*
> *But never will you find friends so true*
> *As those who now say good-by to you.*

"It really rhymed, all of it," said Pippi happily. "I'll learn it by heart and recite it for the people when we sit around the campfires at night."

The children crowded in from all directions to say good-by to Pippi. She raised her hand and asked them to be quiet.

"Children," she said, "hereafter I'll only have little native children to play with. I don't know how we'll amuse ourselves; perhaps we'll play ball with wild

rhinoceroses, and charm snakes, and ride on elephants, and have a swing in the coconut palm outside the door. We'll always manage to pass the time
some way or another." Pippi paused. Both Tommy
and Annika felt that they hated those native children Pippi would play with in the future.

"But," continued Pippi, "perhaps a day will come
during the rainy season, a long and dreary day—
for even if it is fun to run around without your
clothes on a rainy day, you can't do more than get
wet, and when we have got good and wet, perhaps
we'll crawl into my native clay hut, unless the whole
hut has become a mud pile, in which case, of course,
we'll make mud pies. But if the clay hut is still a
clay hut, perhaps we'll crawl in there, and the native
children will say, 'Pippi, please tell us a story.' And
then I will tell them about a little town which lies
far, far away in another part of the world, and about
the children who live there. 'You can't imagine what
nice kids live there,' I'll say to the native children.
'They blow bird whistles, and, best of all, they
know pluttification.' But then perhaps the little
native children will become absolutely desperate
because they don't know any pluttification, and then
what shall I do with them? Well, if worst comes to
worst, I'll take the clay hut to pieces and make a
mud pile out of it, and then we'll bake mud pies and

dig ourselves down into the mud way up to our necks. Then it would be strange if I couldn't get them to think about something else besides pluttification. Thanks, all of you, and good-by so much!"

The children blew a still sadder tune on their bird whistles.

"Pippi, it's time to come aboard," called Captain Longstocking.

"Aye, aye, Captain," called Pippi. She turned to Tommy and Annika. She looked at them.

How strange her eyes look! thought Tommy. His mother had looked just like that once when Tommy had been very, very ill.

Annika lay in a little heap on the packing case. Pippi lifted her in her arms. "Good-by, Annika, good-by," she whispered. "Don't cry."

Annika threw her arms around Pippi's neck and uttered a mournful little cry. "Good-by, Pippi," she sobbed.

Pippi took Tommy's hand and squeezed it hard. Then she ran up the gangplank. A big tear rolled down Tommy's nose. He clenched his teeth, but that didn't help; another tear came. He took Annika's hand, and they stood there and gazed after Pippi. They could see her up on deck, but it is always a little hazy when you try to look through tears.

"Three cheers for Pippi Longstocking!" cried the people on the dock.

"Pull in the gangplank, Fridolf," cried Captain Longstocking. Fridolf did. The *Hoptoad* was ready for her journey to foreign lands.

Then— "No, Papa Efraim," cried Pippi, "I can't do it, I just can't bear to do it!"

"What is it you can't bear to do?" asked Captain Longstocking.

"I can't bear to see anyone on God's green earth crying and being sorry on account of me—least of all Tommy and Annika. Put out the gangplank again. I'm staying in Villa Villekulla."

Captain Longstocking stood silent for a minute. "Do as you like," he said at last. "You always have done that."

Pippi nodded. "Yes, I've always done that," she said quietly.

They hugged each other again, Pippi and her father, so hard that their ribs cracked, and they decided that Captain Longstocking should come very often to see Pippi in Villa Villekulla.

"You know, Papa Efraim," said Pippi, "I think it's best for a child to have a decent home and not sail around on the sea so much and live in native clay huts—don't you think so too?"

"You're right, as always, my daughter," answered

Captain Longstocking. "It is certain that you live a more orderly life in Villa Villekulla, and that is probably best for little children."

"Just so," said Pippi. "It's surely best for little children to live an orderly life, especially if they can order it themselves."

Pippi said good-by to the sailors on the *Hoptoad* and hugged her Papa Efraim once more. Then she lifted her horse in her strong arms and carried him back over the gangplank. The *Hoptoad* weighed anchor, but at the last minute Captain Longstocking remembered something.

"Pippi!" he cried. "You may need some more gold pieces. Here, catch this!"

Then he threw a new suitcase full of gold pieces to Pippi, but unfortunately the *Hoptoad* had got too far away, and the suitcase didn't reach the dock. Plop! Plop! The bag sank. A murmur of dismay went through the crowd, but then there was another plop! It was Pippi diving off the dock. In a few seconds she came up with the suitcase in her teeth. Climbing up on the dock, she brushed away a bit of seaweed that was caught behind her ear.

"Well, now I'm as rich as a troll again," she said.

Things had happened so quickly that Tommy and Annika were bewildered. They stood with wide open mouths and stared at Pippi and the horse and Mr. Nilsson and the suitcase of gold pieces, and the *Hoptoad* in full sail, leaving the harbor.

"Aren't you—aren't you on the boat?" asked Tommy, unable to believe his eyes.

"Make three guesses," said Pippi and wrung the water out of her braids.

She lifted Tommy and Annika, the suitcase, and Mr. Nilsson all up on the horse and swung herself up behind them.

"Back to Villa Villekulla!" she cried in a loud voice.

At last Tommy and Annika understood. Tommy was so happy that he immediately broke out in his favorite song: "Here come the Swedes with a clang and a bang!"

Annika had cried so much that she couldn't stop right away. She still sniffled, but only happy little sniffs that would soon end. Pippi's arms were around her stomach in a strong grip. She felt so safe! Oh, how wonderful everything was!

"What'll we do today, Pippi?" asked Annika when her sniffles had stopped.

"Well, play croquet, perhaps," answered Pippi.

"Goody!" cried Annika, for she knew that even croquet would be quite different when Pippi played.

"Or else—maybe—" said Pippi hesitatingly.

All the children in the little town crowded around the horse to hear what Pippi said.

"Or else," she said, "or else maybe we could run down to the river and practice walking on the water."

"You can't walk on the water. You know that!" said Tommy.

"Oh, it's not impossible," said Pippi. "In Cuba I once met a cabinet maker . . ."

The horse began to gallop, and the little children who crowded around him couldn't hear the rest of the story, but they stood a long, long time, looking after Pippi and her horse galloping toward Villa Villekulla. After a while Pippi and the horse looked like a little speck, far away, and finally they disappeared completely.

ABOUT THE AUTHOR

ASTRID LINDGREN was born on a farm in Sweden and spent a happy childhood there. After her schooling was completed she worked for a time in a newspaper office, was married, and became the mother of a son and daughter. For many years she was an editor in a Swedish publishing house.

When her daughter Karin was seven years old and convalescing from pneumonia, she asked her mother to tell her a story about "Pippi Longstocking." That was the first mention of the character who was to become so famous. Three years later Mrs. Lindgren herself had to stay in bed with an injury to her leg, and she began to write the stories she had been telling Karin and her friends about Pippi. After *Pippi Longstocking* was published in Swedish it was translated into many other languages and became a favorite with children all over the world.

Astrid Lindgren received the Swedish State Award (1956) and the Peace Prize of the German Book Trade (1978), the first children's book writer to do so. Mrs. Lindgren has also won the Hans Christian Andersen Medal (1958), the highest international award in children's literature.

For your reading pleasure ...